WOLF IN THE JUNGLE

A NOVEL BY:

EVAN RAIL

EDITED BY
LIAK NAVE

COVER ILLUSTRATED BY
DAVID KUETTEL

STONE ARCH
ENTERTAINMENT

FUCK NAZIS!

"Wolf in the Jungle"
Written By:
Evan Kail
Stone Arch Entertainment, LLC
Copyright, 2018
United States Copyright Office
Registration #
TXu-2-114-259
8/24/2018

CONTENTS

For Joe and Marty
Plus: my best friend, Steph,
Tracy, Hannah, Lexi,
The kitties...
This book is for the Struzyks.

SALTY WAVES KISSED the frail fishing skipper in cold, choppy bursts. Sweat and ocean stink thickly glazed Lautoro Diaz's skin. He'd braved the rough waters since dawn but had little to show for his efforts. Soon it would be dusk, and now he considered his efforts to be wasted. He wiped the grime from his bushy eyebrows and stared at the ruffled water.

The weather seemed queer for the season. The putrid-colored sky and misdirection of the wind hinted at a storm, yet Lautoro knew it wasn't the right time of year. A religious man his whole life, he wondered if it was a sign.

No other fisher braved the seas this frigid Sunday. Lautoro was all alone out there, just as he liked it best. The silence fed his work ambition and gave him time to reflect.

Fate had taken an eraser to the rest of the Diaz family, starting with his brother, Joaquin, of cancer. Then his sister, Mia, of childbirth. The baby didn't survive, either. Lautoro cursed the name of God before damning himself to a sentence of isolation at sea. There on a floating cross of martyrdom and defeat would he find God again.

One fateful Christmas, he became lost at sea after drinking an entire bottle of rum. A vicious storm swallowed him up, but as the winds screamed and swells threw his tiny boat up and down skyscrapers of water, he found himself laughing through the terror. It was everything he beckoned in pursuit of self-masochism. He had nothing to lose, and if he wanted to die, all he had to do was let go. Strangely his grip held firm, steering the boat against all the odds to safety.

Once he returned to dry land, Lautoro felt invigorated like never before. Something beyond understanding had been with him in those waters. It left an imprint that would change his outlook on life forever.

Thus, the power and intrigue of the deep dark sea. It could heal a soul or steal it just as quickly. Now, decades later, Lautoro had seen all host of bizarre that the ocean had to offer. But nothing- not the late-night scream of an unknown creature far beneath the deep, not the giant ball of light that rose from the water and tore off into the night sky- nothing would shock him like what he was about to witness next.

He had just begun to pack up his gear when he heard it. The water was hiccupping a few yards from his starboard side. He finally perked up when the bubbles became too loud to ignore.

Over the side, he observed a cauldron of heat brewing amidst the jagged waves.

The discolored sky against the water's uneven reflection made the rising shape hard to detect until Lautoro realized the hulking figure was all around him.

The bubbles turned from whispers to jets. With no time to engage the motor, Lautoro hit the deck and covered his head. A large metal frame scraped against his puny wooden boat as it rose from the depths to cast it in shadow.

Lautoro slowly raised his gaze to find not a creature, but a logo just as fearful as any beast from the abyss. He knew the symbol branded on its conning tower all too well. It had been hastily scraped off, but enough remained intact to reveal what it was: Eight black lines, tangled on their side, clasped in the claws of the Iron

Eagle. Lautoro figured the Nazi U-Boat had to be at least eighty feet long.

The U-Boat's hatch creaked open to expel several days of sealed human stench. Lautoro nearly screamed when he saw the man who emerged. His face was wrapped in bandages, rendering him something like an Egyptian mummy.

F resh ocean air after days beneath the surface was something *Kapitän* Kurtz Von Schwangau cherished. It was his first-time seeing daylight in weeks, and his injuries were healing very slowly in the heated, overcrowded U-boat cabin.

It had been a taxing escape to reach the northern Port. Von Schwangau's mutilated face was a testament. Once their payload was secured, they embarked for the other side of the world. Each time they surfaced was hazardous, for the seas were ripe with Allied ships. He was sure they were spotted in the mid-Atlantic, yet not a single depth charge deployed. After that, they only surfaced at night, and just long enough to catch a quick breath.

Von Schwangau gripped the conning tower's railing as he stared up at the swirling sky. He was lost in a daydream until the unexpected mutter of a tiny motor seized his attention. To his amazement, even in these rough seas, there was a fishing boat. He was close enough to trade glances with its captain, certainly a Brazilian.

Von Schwangau had risked everything to keep the cause alive, and now some unknown fisher threatened total obliteration. The man couldn't be allowed to return to shore. With duty in his eyes, Von Schwangau reached for his Mauser C96, undid its strap, and cast the weapon free from its holster. He aimed and squeezed the trigger just once.

The German-made lead sailed through the moist air to find its target. After the bang, nothing could alter its course. It entered the back of Lautoro's skull and exited cleanly out of his left eye socket.

His limp body slumped over the edge and was swallowed by the sea, while his unmanned boat slammed into a wave and capsized.

Von Schwangau turned to his *Kapitänleutnant* and commanded, "Prepare to dive. We resurface for the river mouth after dark."

The hatch closed with loud steel slam and slipped back beneath the waves. Lautoro's body descended alongside the metal leviathan. He would never know he'd died to protect a secret that threatened to destroy the very foundations of justice forever.

CHAPTER 1

MARCH 1953 - BUDAPEST, HUNGARY

THE BURLAP SACK emitted a loud metallic clang under the shaky cobblestone path. The cab driver wondered what his passenger's contents could be, but he knew better than to ask. It went against every part of his code. His only job was to drive, not ask questions. Still, he couldn't help but ponder.

The passenger in the back was in his mid-fifties, with blond hair and piercing blue eyes. The man was Herman Kline, and unbeknownst to the driver, the bounty on his head was a kingly sum.

Herman rested a nervous hand over the sack to mute its suspicious noise. They rode without conversation, the cab occasionally creaking or scraping against stone.

Herman looked down at his wrinkly hands. In the haste of chase, time had flown off the clock. Now it had all come down to this. After eight years of shameful retreat, Herman was at the gates of freedom. The upcoming exchange at the jewelers would be his passage, and in a few short weeks, he'd be reunited with his brothers again.

Herman's smile wilted as he fidgeted in the grimy seat. How he missed his state-issued Mercedes Benz W31. He longed for the days when he used to motor beyond the camp's walls and whip through the winding roads of Oranienburg. The war was deafening, and only motoring through that curvy forest pass could deliver his mind peace. There was a particular spot he'd frequent to clean his father's old Dreyse M1907. It was there Herman buried a different forlorn treasure. He'd jeopardized everything to sneak back into Germany and retrieve it. Now that it was securely in his possession, nothing could stand in his way.

Or could it? Herman wondered. He scowled at paranoia. Undoubtedly the hardest part was behind him.

When the cab came to a stop in front of a jewelers, Herman counted out the exact amount for the fare and handed it to the driver. The driver hissed over his stymied tip, but Herman paid no mind. He stepped out with the heavy sack slung over his shoulder and shut the door. The driver angrily drove away with a parting horn blare.

Herman didn't even hear it. Everything had come down to these next few moments. The world around him turned mute. As he took those steps up to the jeweler's front door, memories came rushing back:

During the war, savagery was like a drug. Every time he shot an enemy of the state, his twisted tastes came alive. He loved it. His men loved it. They'd been wolves, and the ethnic plague was a carcass savored with ravenous zeal. His love for bloodlust earned a glowing commendation from the hierarchy. He was transferred to Sachsenhausen, where his demented talents truly shined. It was an effort that earned him the title of *Kommandant*.

But irony would steal the last laugh. The war effort fell apart, and once Herman's men began deserting, he realized with horror what would come next: He'd be a war criminal. To await arrest was to accept besmirched death. So, he shed his medals, shaved his hair, and left his honor as a German soldier shattered.

Thrice, Herman was apprehended, and thrice he managed to slip away. The last instance was far too close. Five years prior, a British soldier recognized him in a public bathroom in Rome. The soldier grabbed Herman by the arm and pulled him into a stall. Before he could draw his gun, Herman slammed a pen into the soldier's jugular.

He slumped the soldier onto the toilet and hung his bleeding neck between his legs over the bowl as to catch all the blood. Since then, Herman suffered several close calls, but nobody had ever managed to fire a shot.

Just as he reached for the jeweler's door handle, a terrible feeling crept back. He froze and nervously peered around. There was nobody suspicious in sight.

Little did Herman realize he had good reason to fear.

⸻

"Rabbit is in sight," Uzziel Abraham confirmed into a short-wave radio. The muscular 61-year-old aimed a scoped Russian SKS-45 freehand from a second story window. He hated Russian guns, especially this one. Even with a scope, the SKS was bad at 100 yards, terrible at 250, and beyond 500, it wasn't even worth taking the shot. But if apprehended inside Soviet territory, Nesher Unit couldn't leave any trace of its true American origins. Foreign guns were a necessity for this reason. "Clear for go."

"Streets are free of mice, Raptor. Wait for rabbit's confirmation," Nadir Horowitz replied. She stood across from the jewelers watching Herman like a hawk. As Nesher Unit's intelligence wiz, it was on her to confirm the target. However, this was her very first time operating in the field, and she had to beg for deployment on such a risky mission.

"C'mon, look at me," she muttered. Then, as if he heard her, Herman's blue eyes bore directly into hers. Her heart practically leaped through her mouth. "Rabbit is confirmed," she breathed.

Uzziel's crosshairs fixed right on Herman's temple. One bullet would pop his head like a grape... If he could hit the target.

Herman turned the knob and opened the door.

"Eagle, our window is closing!" Uzziel said. His finger was wrapped around the trigger waiting to pull.

Inside the back of a nearby Citroën H van, Bar-Yochai Ginzberg, Herschel Levine, and Vadim Kohn waited for orders.

Nesher Unit's commander, Avery Thompson, shook his head and said into the radio, "Stand down, Raptor. We're taking him alive." He nodded to his men and sent the van into a symphony of snapping ammunition magazines and cocking guns.

Uzziel removed his finger from the trigger and replied, "Copy that, Eagle." His sights remained locked on Herman as he disappeared off the street.

———

The air inside of the jewelers was dusty and stale. It didn't take a detective to see very few people visited this particular vendor, but given the nature of his real business, Jinter Boozis relied on quality over quantity. To the laypeople of Budapest, he was a quiet shopkeeper who attracted very few patrons. In reality, he was a silent king with the power to acquire anything his clients sought. The precious stones on display in his storefront were a dismal fraction of his real operations.

Herman meandered around the vacant store, his steps echoing with the creaky wooden floorboards. When he turned around, he found the lanky, fair-skinned Jinter had not just appeared but was donning a Nazi salute to greet him.

Seeing the gesture, Herman nearly wept. "My God. No one's given me a proper greeting in ages," he mused in German, returning the salute with another.

Jinter lowered his arm and said in German, "This way, please."

Herman followed Jinter into a private back office. "I can't discuss much, even in private like this," Jinter explained. "But Herman, once you see what your brothers have accomplished, you'll be beside yourself."

Herman remained cool as he rested the heavy sack on Jinter's desk.

Jinter withdrew a loupe from a drawer and said, "First, I'll grade quality. Then I'll run the numbers factoring expenses, smelting fees, market value, etcetera. Only then will I give you a price. I support the cause, but I'm running a business as well. I will give you the passport and get you to your destination, but the amount I pay beyond-"

The two froze when they heard the entry bell jingle. A masculine-sounding voice called "Hello?" in Russian.

Herman picked up the burlap sack and tailed behind Jinter.

Jinter peered around the corner to discover four men who looked strong enough to crush diamonds. "May I help you?" he asked in a soft Hungarian tongue. With a little luck, a language barrier might banish the men with ease.

"Special Police. A man just came in here. We need to speak with him immediately," Herschel replied in perfect Hungarian. Between the six of them, there were very few languages absent from Nesher Unit's dialectic arsenal.

Jinter felt Herman's icy fingers digging into his arm. He nudged him to deflect Herman's worry. "I'm sorry, gentlemen, but you're mistaken. Nobody has been in the store all day," Jinter said.

Thompson was in no mood for games. They were deep inside hostile territory and had to get out as quickly as they could. He fought the urge to draw his gun and storm into the back. "Herschel, tell him we mean it," he muttered under his breath in Hebrew. Since all of Nesher Unit's activity was covert, English, in front of any witnesses, was strictly forbidden.

Herschel growled in Hungarian, "Listen, jeweler. We are not the people to play games. If he's hiding in the back, make no mistake we will take you in and charge you with obstruction. We might even-"

Herman sprang into view with his father's Dreyse jammed against Jinter's temple.

Jinter shrieked when he felt the cold metal barrel pressed against his soft, supple skin. He pleaded to Herman in German, but his words fell on deaf ears, for primal instinct hijacked Herman beyond reason.

"Drop the gun, Herman!" Thompson shouted in German.

Everyone had drawn a weapon now. Thompson knew he had a split-second to make up his mind. He wanted to see Herman tried, shamed, and hanged like the beast he was. However secrecy reigned supreme, and a gunfight in the middle of Budapest was anything but.

"Herman, step away from the jeweler, and we'll guarantee a fair trial," Thompson pleaded. He was starting to think a bullet to Herman's brain might be their only chance to issue justice.

Herman never looked so furious in his life. "Trial by Jew?! I think not!" he shouted. He threw Jinter forward, raised his gun, and unleashed a volley of lead.

Thompson and Vadim dove in opposite directions, while Herschel and Bar-Yochai held their ground and returned fire.

Bullets flew through the air, shredding Jinter in the crossfire. He was a mangled, bloody mess before he even hit the ground.

Herman hit nothing but storefront emptying the eight rounds in his pistol. As he turned to flee, his burlap sack was slit open by a hot bullet. Gold teeth spilled all over the floor and colored the room in gleaming light. He dove to the ground and stuffed his pockets before scuttling out the back door.

Everyone tore off after Herman except Vadim, who bent down to inspect one of the gold fillings. Disgust plagued his face. He muttered a Hebrew prayer, pocketed the filling, and ran out the back.

Jinter leaked blood all over the floor. He knew he only had a few moments left. He fished a cigarette into his mouth, lit it and then tossed the lighter onto an antique chair. The old piece of wood quickly caught fire. He puffed out his last few breaths while staring at the growing flames. His clandestine clientele would rest easy, for nobody would retrieve a single secret from his deathbed.

Inside the Fiat, Herman leaked blood everywhere. His useless wounded arm forced him to steer with his knees as he reached over to shift gears with his left hand. He had one spare magazine left. He ejected the empty Dreyse clip and inserted a new one.

The busy road spun out of the city to reveal an expansive countryside devoid of traffic. Once Herman fancied himself clear, he allowed his emotions to unfurl. The gold teeth had been his only way to get overseas. It took the cause years to find someone resourceful like Jinter. All Herman had left were a few handfuls of filings, and it wouldn't be nearly enough for the trek across the ocean, let alone a new passport. He'd have to craft an entirely new plan from scratch.

Herman considered the men who thwarted his transaction. They'd caught him off guard and were extremely well-armed. He'd grossly underestimated the Jews who hungered for vengeance. Until his wounds could heal, he'd have to find a safe place to lay low and hide.

Herman wondered where he might go next. His thoughts hardly had time to mature before a bullet zinged through the back and exited out the Fiat's windshield. He looked in his rearview mirror and recognized two men from the jewelry store barreling up in a convertible.

A second bullet ripped through the back window and shot the rearview mirror off.

Herman slammed on the gas. Survivalist adrenaline coached him through agony to keep him lucid. He grabbed his gun and carelessly waved it out the window to return fire.

While Herman threw away slugs, Bar-Yochai aimed with proper care. Each time he squeezed the trigger, his intended target was hit. He first wanted to alert Herman of their presence. Next, he wished to salt Herman with fear.

Herman's bullets zinged past Bar-Yochai's head, but Bar-Yochai's aim remained steady. He carefully squeezed the Makarov's trigger.

Air rushing down the barrel created a rattling effect against the

Makarov's chamber. The firing pin struck the bullet at an odd angle, launching it in an uneven trajectory. But Bar-Yochai knew pistols like a butcher knew a cleaver. He'd calibrated for the air vibration without even thinking.

The bullet launched from the barrel and careened toward the Fiat's left-rear tire. It ripped through the rubber and sent shards flying up into the car's undercarriage.

In all his years of running, Herman had never once been in a car chase. The stately Mercedes Benz of the S.S. made for grand show, but lousy evasive motoring. His driving skill was less than novice, and his poor decision to oversteer reflected that.

The Fiat spun helplessly out of control and careened off the road. Herman's oversteer put it at such a poor angle that as it went into the ditch, it flipped in a tangle of crunching metal.

The MG came to a graceful halt a few dozen feet behind the ruined Fiat. Bar-Yochai and Thompson climbed out of the MG and slowly approached the steaming wreck.

"Careful, Bar. He might have another gun," Thompson warned.

"Then I'll blast his hand off," Bar-Yochai growled. He could faintly hear Herman's weak coughs coming from inside the ruined Fiat. He pointed the gun and peered inside.

Herman hung from his seatbelt like a carcass suspended from a slaughterhouse meat hook. Blood streamed down his face and collected in a pool on the roof beneath him.

Bar-Yochai noticed a few gold teeth scattered about the cabin. Herman's blood had speckled most of them, an irony Bar-Yochai took exceptional pleasure at witnessing. He leaned in and undid Herman's seatbelt, causing Herman to fall with an "Oof!"

Bar-Yochai yanked the flimsy Herman right out the window and threw him before Thompson's feet.

Herman looked up dazzled and dumbfounded. He was finally at the doorstep of inescapable justice.

Thompson kneeled and looked Herman dead in the eyes to

address him in German. "Well, well, well. *Kommandant* Kline. We've been after you for quite some time-"

Without warning, Herman defiantly spat in Thompson's face.

Thompson wiped it off with a smile. "Now I'm thinking all you little Krauts had a chat back in the Wolf's Lair about how when you were caught, you'd spit in their faces. Every single one of you does it. Do you know what we do back?"

Thompson extracted a small leather pack from his cargo pant leg and opened it up to show Herman a syringe full of green liquid.

"Your old pal Dr. Mengele concocted this. It's quite nasty. This serum stimulates all of the body's pain receptors at once." Thompson jammed the needle into Herman's arm and pumped the liquid into his veins.

A terrified look crept across the old Nazi's face before he suddenly erupted with screams. Of all the agony they'd seen over their military careers, neither Thompson nor Bar-Yochai had ever heard a man scream with such torment. They winced for their ears as they held Herman down.

Herman writhed like a snake. It was as if lightning were shooting through his entire body.

Bar-Yochai kept Herman's arms pinned with his knees and used his hands to hold his mouth shut.

"Now that we have your attention, Herman, I'd like to introduce myself. My name is Avery Thompson, and this is my associate, Bar-Yochai Ginzburg. We're part a little unit that deals with... well, let's say we've met plenty of your friends. We know you're rendezvousing with more, and we know the jeweler was helping. We just don't know how many or where."

Herman's muffled cries were loud enough to merit Thompson shouting, "Now you've only got about three minutes until your heart gives out, so I'll make it very simple. Tell us what we want to know. I'll inject you with the antidote, and then we'll take you into custody to stand trial. Or you can die right here on the side of the road. What'll it be?"

Thompson nodded for Bar-Yochai to remove his hand from Herman's mouth. Through his screams, he managed to squeal "Vermin!"

They could hear sirens now. Bar-Yochai turned in their direction and said, "Thompson, we need to disappear."

Thompson held up a finger, ferociously staring down at Herman in disbelief. "Do you really want to die like this, Herman?"

Herman's vocal cords were withered beyond capacity to reply. All he could do was scowl with boiling fury.

Thompson sighed and said, "Very well. I hear it's Chanukah every day in Nazi Hell, Herman. Have some *Manischewitz* on us when you get there. Bar, pat him down before he shits himself."

Herman started to seize. His eyes rolled back into his head.

Bar-Yochai patted him up and down. All he found was petty cash and gold fillings. He tossed it aside and turned him over.

"Oh, fuck me!" Bar-Yochai shrieked, plugging his nose at the stench of feces.

"Keep searching," Thompson said.

Bar-Yochai grimaced as he slid his hands into Herman's soiled pant pockets.

"More cash," Bar-Yochai fumed, throwing a wad of brown-spattered money that scattered when it hit the ground. He wiped off his hands and scoffed an utterance of revolted Hebrew.

"Dammit," Thompson muttered. The sirens drew closer. When he looked at the soiled cash blowing in the wind, he noticed an unknown piece of paper was among it.

"Hey, wait a sec," he said. He dashed over and snatched up the scrap.

"What is it?" Bar-Yochai asked, wiping his hands off on his black tactical pants.

The wrinkled parchment bore two hand-written numbers:

-1.83; -56.17

"I don't know, but maybe we're in luck," Thompson said. He tucked the paper into his pocket. "Let's get the hell out of here."

"What about the body?"

"A John Doe with no papers is the Red's problem now."

"It's a loose end, T. The Sovs keep records on Nazi fugitives too. It won't take long to figure out his true identity."

"Maybe you're right," Thompson said. He whipped out his pistol and discharged the entire clip into Herman's face. "There. Let's see them identify that."

"You're a real class act," Bar-Yochai said. The two hopped in the MG and took off before the sirens were upon them.

CHAPTER 2

*I*F ONLY *T*HOMPSON *had let me take the shot,* Uzziel thought to himself. With sirens blaring all over the city, Nesher Unit's plan looked wholly undone. A carefully-rehearsed retreat would be their only shot at escape.

A Citroën H van parked half a block from the jewelers was the first rendezvous point. A safehouse hidden in the attic of an abandoned warehouse on the other side of town was the second. Once reunited, Nesher Unit would hold tight and wait for extraction.

Uzziel finished packing up his rifle. He clipped the case shut and muttered, "Raptor exiting next," into his radio. He fled down a fire escape, threw on a sheepskin hat, and melted into the crowd gathering outside the jewelers.

Broken glass littered the street. The store itself was now fully ablaze with smoke spewing high into the air. A few Soviet authorities were already sealing off the perimeter.

With his head bowed low, Uzziel prowled past the jewelers. He could see the Citroën at the end of the block. Nadir was walking parallel to him on the opposite side of the street. She was like the daughter he never had. He'd saved her from the Nazis and made her his protégé, and if anyone made a move to stop her, he'd throw every precaution to the dogs. Anything to keep her safe.

They were only a hundred paces from the van. All Uzziel had to do was keep walking. He'd been trained to know that retreat meant keep your head down, maintain a low profile, and avoid eye contact with everyone. But he was still human, and the whole incident had left his instincts wilted. With just fifty feet to go, a young Soviet police officer running toward the scene unexpectedly bumped shoulders with him. The impact caused Uzziel to drop his rifle case, which split wide open. The rifle pieces loudly clanged as they spilled out on the street for all to see.

The officer gaped. He hardly expected to encounter any excitement, let alone a world-class military unit on his first year of duty. He drew his sidearm once the glistening rifle pieces registered with his brain.

The maneuver spooked Uzziel to take evasive action. He reached for his own Makarov pistol.

The officer panicked and fired a lone shot into the ground near Uzziel's foot. Life-or-death training hijacked Uzziel's body and caused him to return fire.

The crowd screamed and scattered. The officer erupted blood as he caught two shots to the neck and one to the chest. He fired off one final shot as his body went limp.

The officer's bullet found a warm home right inside of Uzziel's lower intestine. He keeled to the ground. The Makarov slid free from his hand and landed in a puddle of his own blood.

Across the street, Nadir watched powerlessly. She bolted over and scraped her mentor off the pavement. His bloodshot eyes were drowning. Words eluded him.

Nadir looked over at the Soviet. She could see he was dead.

The Citroën screeched to a curbside stop right next to them. The back doors flung open. Vadim, now sporting a black ski mask, screamed "Get in!" in Hebrew.

Nadir grabbed Uzziel's Makarov and fired a single shot into the air to scatter the straggling onlookers. Vadim jumped out. Together they loaded Uzziel into the van and then took off.

"Herschel! Keep this thing stable!" Vadim scolded as he stripped away Uzziel's shirt. A single bullet hole two inches left of his belly-button spewed blood like a geyser. Gravity threw them tumbling with each aggressive turn.

"Slow down! He's dying back here!" Nadir screamed.

"If I go any slower, all of us are fucked!" Herschel roared. The van smacked a parked car the instant he finished his words.

Uzziel screwed up his face as the impact wrung out more blood. Nadir and Vadim were covered red.

"Uzzie! Stay with us!" Nadir pleaded. She was incapable of helping a person she loved dearly, a feeling she'd known too many times in her twenty-six years of life. She squeezed his hand.

Vadim firmly held a rag over the wound. "He's going into hypovolemic shock," he said. "Uzzie, can you hear me?! Uzzie?!"

Uzziel's teary eyes darted every which way. He tried to speak, but gasps stole the place of his words.

"Herschel, how far out are we from the safe house?" Vadim said.

"Five minutes. I'm going to drop you guys off and ditch this rig," Herschel replied.

"His blood pressure is plummeting," Vadim said. He was a trained combat medic, but even battlefields weren't subject to the burden of mobile physics. He could only apply pressure and keep his patient lucid through talking. "There are medical supplies at the safe house. Just hold on, Uzzie! You're going to be fine!" He couldn't mask the doubt laced in his voice. He slid a finger against Uzziel's wrist and checked his pulse.

The beat was getting weak.

CHAPTER 3

DRIVING WAS one of Avery Thompson's greatest pleasures in life. As a youth, he ran with a tough crowd on Brooklyn's east side and got a knack for boosting cars. His troublesome hobby manifested into something far more sinister when a local kingpin received word of his talents. It was the Great Depression, and everyone's pockets were bleeding. Thompson served as a getaway driver for no less than six robberies. Despite the risk, he confidently knew Brooklyn like the back of his hand, and whenever he got behind the wheel, Avery Thompson was a force to be reckoned.

However, this was neither Brooklyn, nor a simple getaway. Every Soviet badge within a hundred miles was probably searching for them. Thompson ground his teeth as his sweaty hands tightly gripped the MG's steering wheel.

"Do you even know where you're going?" Bar-Yochai asked.

Thompson took his eyes off the road to stare at his soldier. "New rule. You shoot, I drive," Thompson replied.

Bar-Yochai knew an order when he heard one. Still, it was hard to ignore how badly everything had gone to hell. "We really should have stuffed Herman in the trunk. It's a loose end," Bar-Yochai said.

"He never would have fit."

"Oh, I could have made him."

"With the way we left Kline, the only thing the Soviets will able to confirm was that he was a human male," Thompson said.

They skimmed the outskirts of town far from the sirens. When Thompson turned onto a road that led further south, Bar-Yochai objected, "Isn't the safe house on the northern part of the city?"

"This car is too hot. We're going to roll it in the water and go from there."

Bar-Yochai reached under the seat and found a woman's bonnet. He tied it over his head to go with the oversized sunglasses stashed in the glove box.

"Are you nuts? You're going to get us stopped for immorality," Thompson said.

"Are you calling me fat, Thompson?" Bar-Yochai said.

"No, I'm calling you an ugly man poorly disguised as an even uglier woman. Take that damn thing off."

Bar-Yochai undid the bonnet to let it go flying in the wind. The MG wrapped around a tight curve. When it emerged from the bend, Thompson and Bar-Yochai traded uneasy expressions.

Two military trucks with Soviet flags painted on their hoods were approaching in the oncoming lane.

Bar-Yochai thumbed the safety off his pistol.

"Don't even look at them," Thompson warned. "Maybe nobody reported this car yet."

The Soviet trucks fanned out to block the road.

"Fuck," Thompson said, slowing the car.

They came to a dead stop a few hundred feet in front of the blockade. Soviet soldiers unloaded from the trucks and spread across the length of the road.

"I'm thinking they got the report," Bar-Yochai said.

When Thompson saw Bar-Yochai readying his gun, he said again, "Listen to me. Do-not-shoot."

"T, we're about to be shredded by Russian lead."

"Every bullet we trade is a nail in our coffin if we make it stateside."

"I'd rather be buried there than there," Bar-Yochai said.

"Take out a grenade," Thompson said.

Bar-Yochai looked at him doubtfully and extracted a hand grenade from his cargo pant pocket. "You'll never hit them from this range."

The commander of the Soviets yelled in Russian, "Exit the vehicle, slowly, with your arms above your heads! You have until the count of five. One... Two... Three..."

"Give me that," Thompson said, snatching the grenade out of Bar-Yochai's hand. He pulled the pin, tossed it, whipped the wheel, and slammed his foot into the gas.

The MG spun around and took off right as the grenade landed in between them on the road.

The Soviets got just a few shots off before the grenade exploded. By the time they got back on their feet, the MG had vanished.

They left discretion dead in the dust. Thompson raced off a busy main road, cut through a narrow alleyway, and emerged in a bustling market square. "Clear the way," he instructed.

Bar-Yochai raised his pistol and fired off two shots. The market emptied within seconds.

They prowled through the desolate market and then slithered into another alley network. The MG now boasted a cracked windshield and dozens of bullet holes. Thompson suspected one of the Soviet slugs had done some damage, for the car began losing power. He still had no idea where they'd find a body of water deep enough to sink it in.

"We might have to abandon the car outright," Thompson said. "I can feel it's about to give out on us."

A panicked Russian voice shouted at them from behind. They turned around to witness a uniformed Soviet soldier furiously waving for backup. He freed his pistol of its holster and opened fire.

Thompson hit the gas it as Bar-Yochai returned fire. The Soviet dropped when a bullet winged him. But as he fell back, five more took his place to keep shooting.

The MG escaped with a dozen new bullet holes and finally gave out as they turned onto a busy road.

"Okay, plan B!" Thompson yelled. He jumped out the MG and started running down the street.

"What's plan B?" Bar-Yochai called after him.

"Don't fall behind!" Thompson shouted.

They ran blindly through the alleys until they came across a brick building that bore a wooden door. Thompson kicked the door in and pulled Bar-Yochai inside.

They barricaded the door with a piece of wood. Then they descended a metal staircase into an old basement, where they found a locked door at the bottom.

Thompson and Bar-Yochai exchanged looks and started kicking in unison. On their fourth kick, the door broke. They stepped inside a dusty boiler room.

Bar-Yochai took out his lighter and produced a flame to illuminate the room.

"Look for a drainage system," Thompson said. The two got on their hands and knees, scouring cobwebs along the floor and ceiling.

"Thompson," Bar-Yochai said. He wrapped his hands around a storm drain and ripped it off with a grunt. "After you."

CHAPTER 4

THE TREK to the safe house was the longest five minutes of Uzziel's life. Every turn, every bump, every joule of force felt like a million pins stabbing his stomach over and over again. He'd passed out and regained consciousness over half a dozen times. Each instance sent his head spiraling with memories:

He remembered his father's old war stories. There were not many American Jews who served in those days, and his father's bravery had been a point of pride for Uzziel. He had a medal which he showed to Uzziel on occasion, telling him, "One day it will be yours to wear if you prove yourself."

On a sunny Sunday after synagogue service, he snuck into his father's bedroom and dug the medal out. He held it in his frail young hands and almost put it on. But then he stopped short. To wear it in secrecy was to forsake his father's challenge. It would sully the day when he put it on for real. He ran his fingers along its shiny golden surface and placed the medal back in its box.

"Uzziel," spoke a woman's voice from far away. At first, he thought it was his mother. Then he remembered she'd been dead for decades. He returned to consciousness and found the worried faces of Nadir and Vadim peering over him.

He reached for his father's medal and felt it sitting securely around his neck. Now was the time to prove his worthiness. If nothing else, he had to be strong for Nadir. When his unit found her hiding in '44, she was on the brink of starvation. He nursed her, got her stateside to a relative's in Chicago, and guided her first to citizenship, then to the U.S. Army. He'd prepared Nadir for a situation just like this, but training and reality felt worlds apart.

Another bump in the road sent Uzziel careening back into the void.

He remembered his first kill. He could still taste the man's blood as it spattered into his open mouth.

It was shortly after they landed in Europe at the start of '18. He'd been clearing an empty building when the German soldier snuck up on him with piano wire. Right as the wire wrapped tightly around Uzziel's neck, he hip-checked the German and threw him over his shoulder. He had him pinned on his back but lost footing when the German kicked out his knee. The German mounted Uzziel and managed to get the wire around his neck again. Uzziel's shouts for help went mute as the wire became tight.

The room faded to darkness. Just when Uzziel considered the fight lost, he reached for his knife and plunged it into the man's temple. The German's hazel-colored eyes went blank as blood leaked from the wound and dribbled into Uzziel's mouth. He could still remember the warm metallic taste.

He could taste it again, only this time, the blood was his own. He awoke in a dim room lit by a single table light. He looked at his arm and found a makeshift IV jammed into the vein.

Herschel stood in the doorway with folded arms and a firm face. Nicknamed "The Hammer," he was a decorated soldier who shied from little. Seeing his brother in arms so gravely injured visibly chipped away from his hardened psyche.

A bright flash stole Uzziel's attention. He looked over to observe Vadim drawing a flame across a blade.

Vadim looked down at Uzziel and said, "You picked a shit time to wake up, pal. We've got to get that bullet out."

Uzziel felt too weak for words. He knew any one of them would gladly trade places, were it that simple. He wasn't sure if he trusted Vadim more for his devoted loyalty as a friend or his prowess as a surgeon. In any event, whatever happened next, he was in good hands.

Vadim slid the hot blade into Uzziel's stomach and sent pain radiating throughout his entire body. His overloaded nerve receptors yanked his eyes back into his head and kicked him into another dream spell.

Just like his father, Uzziel went career military. After the second World War, Uzziel bounced around various branches of the U.S. military, eventually landing a joint-officer position with the newly-commissioned Israeli forces. He considered it a mistake almost immediately. He hadn't a doubt in his mind the cause he served was just. The only problem resided in his comrades. The unit he'd been assigned to consisted of eleven other men. Three were so dumb that he secretly considered them meat shields. Two were psychopaths who couldn't be trusted. Then there was the team's commander, Etan, a man so reckless, Uzziel constantly wondered how he eluded court-martial.

He'd sought transfer back to the states twice, and both times he was denied. Only when he threatened to leave the military outright did an opportunity present itself. A Jewish-American General named Alan Fink was forming a small, covert unit, and looking for recruits. After a brief meeting with Avery Thompson, the man who'd be leading the group, Uzziel knew escaped Nazis was a bone well worth the chase. Since then he'd killed for Nesher Unit, and bled for it, too. Just never like this.

Uzziel awoke to see Nadir standing over his head holding down his arms. Bedsheets bound his legs. Herschel was gone. Vadim ignored the pain of his patient and continued the operation.

"Almost got it," Uzziel heard him say. He could feel the blade digging around inside him. The knife touched the bullet. The pain felt so incredible that it flung Uzziel back into unconsciousness.

She was a beauty Uzziel would have fought a thousand wars to win. The year was 1933 when he noticed her from the other side of the congregation. The Rabbi walked past with the Torah when their eyes aligned. For Uzziel that first gaze was as mystifying as staring up at a cloudless night sky. He felt his iron heart skip a beat in utter awe of her.

It was a fast-blossoming love. But mere days before they planned to elope, she was struck by a taxi cab and killed.

Uzziel hadn't seen her in decades, yet somehow, she was standing in front of him as clear as day. When he tried to speak, his mouth felt glued shut.

Uzziel's eyes jolted open when he heard the clang of the bullet dropping into the metal bucket. Thompson and Bar-Yochai were there now, talking with Vadim and Nadir. Herschel was still nowhere to be seen. Everyone's mouths were moving, but their words eluded his ears.

Then, in the doorway, he saw her again. *Impossible*, he thought. *It has to be!* And yet, there she stood. It was the twinkle in her stare which assured Uzziel his eyes weren't cheating him. She motioned for Uzziel to join her.

Uzziel got up and took a few steps to follow before turning to look back. He saw his own mortal body lying on the bed. His friends were frantically screaming into his unresponsive ears. Herschel raced into the room and ran right through him.

Uzziel observed the scene of his own death. Tears streaked down Nadir's face. Vadim threw the knife aside and furiously began chest compressions. Herschel powerlessly stood by in paralyzed shock, eyes swelling with rare tears.

Uzziel turned away from his body. Now that he'd seen his love again, he felt at peace. He remembered hearing death was a cold business, but warmth crept through every fiber of his being. He knew

Nesher Unit would never be the same without him. He almost returned to his body, until he heard the beauty calling his name.

Uzziel turned to face the doorway again. She wasn't alone. Beside her stood every single person Uzziel had ever lost. All were smiling and waiting for him to join them. Though they'd never hear it, Uzziel bid his friends "Farewell." Then he took his long-lost love by the hand and left this world forever.

CHAPTER 5

SIRENS HUMMED all through the night. Unbeknownst to Nesher Unit, their mission fell on the tenth consecutive day of civil unrest, and the brutal slaying of a police officer sparked utter hysteria. The city was on total lockdown, and all Nesher Unit could do was wait. Given the harsh turn of events, nobody was in a hurry to do anything except mourn.

There had been many gunfights in the three years since Nesher Unit's inception. There were countless injuries, but never a casualty. The thought of replacing one of his teammates was something Thompson intentionally kept far from his mind. Watching Uzziel expire sent the bitter truth of mortality blasting through his psyche.

Their hideout was constructed in secrecy by Central Intelligence in its ever-expanding wargames against communism. It boasted enough supplies to last weeks and even housed a working shower. It also bore a large freezer, something Thompson took no pleasure in when he ordered Uzziel be wrapped in bedsheets and stored inside. With no place to bury their fallen comrade, they'd been forced to put him on ice until extraction.

Bar-Yochai wanted to talk shop right away. Mere hours after

Uzziel had died, he cornered Thompson while everyone else slept and said, "We need to go over what happened."

"Not now," Thompson said.

"Thompson, if we don't have the next step firmly in place before we make contact with Fink, we might as well kiss Nesher Unit goodbye."

Thompson furrowed his expression. "No shit, Bar. This was a disaster in every sense. I realize what you're saying, but right now none of us can think straight. Give it a few days, alright? God knows we're not going anywhere any time soon."

Bar-Yochai had no reply. He nodded obediently and then quietly withdrew.

A few days passed. Herschel uncovered a few bottles of liquor stocked in a cabinet. Bar-Yochai joined him in an odyssey of whiskey and sorrow. Thomson grounded them when their drunken movements became a cause for alarm.

Nadir kept to herself, crying her eyes out every moment of privacy she got. Finally, once she felt numb, her mourning took the form of forlorn silence. Uzziel had been a guardian angel from the moment he entered her life. His death was an emotional wound she thought she might never fully heal from.

Though he felt it too, Vadim reframed from exhibiting overt emotion. He took to his pastime of artwork, sketching out drawing after drawing, only to crumple each one up and toss it away.

Thompson's feelings remained ambivalent. It was paramount to demonstrate strength in the face of defeat, yet sorrow plagued his subconscious. He participated with everyone in mental effort to distract himself. He drank with Bar-Yochai and Herschel, shed a few tears with Nadir, and even attempted drawing with Vadim. Though he wasn't nearly as skilled, he found art to be the most therapeutic. It was a long, slow, and painful time as Nesher Unit mourned.

Early in the morning of their third-day hiding, the radio crackled a Morse code signal. Nadir heard it first. "Guys! Get in here!" she hissed.

Everyone scrambled to gather around the radio. Nadir listened and decrypted the crackles to spell out a new radio frequency. She held it up to Thompson and said, "Change it over."

Thompson adjusted the dial.

A second Morse code frequency began to play on the new channel. Nadir wrote a few letters down and said dreadfully, *"M- Four."*

They were the exact words Thompson did not want to hear. In events like these where the airwaves could be under surveillance, Nesher Unit relied on a brief set of codes to communicate with headquarters. "M-Four" meant a situation so hostile, all they could do was ping once to acknowledge they understood.

Nadir continued to translate. "X. Two. X-B," she announced. It meant, "Stay put. It's a shit storm, and now we're figuring out an extraction." It signaled they could be stuck for weeks.

Then the frequency went static. Thompson said, "Get cozy, everyone."

"It doesn't make sense," Vadim said. "We did a lot of damage. But not M-Four level. For Pete's sake, the Poland operation wasn't even an M-Four. What did you two do?" he asked, looking at Thompson and Bar-Yochai.

Thompson shook his head. "It doesn't matter. If we hadn't gone after Herman like that, he would have slipped away, and all this would have been for nothing. We got our man. It just came at a high price."

"The real question now is, how long will the Soviets search for us?" Nadir wondered.

"Central Intelligence went to a lot of trouble constructing this place. They can look all year. They'll never find us," Thompson assured. "We just need to hang tight."

"Once we do get back, what exactly are you planning to tell General Fink?" Vadim asked.

Thompson brooded on a reply. Only in hindsight did it occur to him leaving Herman's body to rot in the dirt indeed might have been a mistake. Even though he was certain he'd left Herman unidentifiable, Bar-Yochai was right- it was still a loose end. A Soviet police officer killed on red soil was bad enough. Telling the truth about Herman's body wouldn't do Nesher Unit any favors in the post-operational report. Nesher Unit was General Fink's brainchild, but even he had limits as to what he'd tolerate.

"I'll think of something," Thompson meekly said.

"I don't doubt it. I just want to know, who are you saying shot first?" Vadim was a man of many expressions. The questioning look on his face was Thompson's least favorite.

"The Sov tried to nab Uzziel as he was retreating to the van. Uzziel fought back. Sov shot him in the gut. Uzziel retaliated to stop him from shooting again."

"That's not quite how it happened," began Nadir, "But I'll back it up. I was across the street. Uzziel didn't have a choice."

"You should have let him take the shot on Herman when he had the chance, Thompson," Vadim said.

Everyone went dead quiet. Vadim realized his error after the words left his lips. Thompson fought every urge to scream back. He swallowed his rage and calmly said, "None of us would be sitting here if I had. We would have been swarmed and arrested."

"Sorry," Vadim said.

"Look, there's no playbook for what we're all feeling. It hurts more than anything, but now we have a test to endure. We either stay focused and stay together, or else Uzziel truly died for nothing."

Thompson took a few slow paces around the room. He reached in his pocket and continued, "I have something to show you all. I didn't want to talk about it for a few days, but we have a decision to make." He laid the parchment stolen from Herman on the center of the table.

"The hell's that?" asked Vadim.

"I plucked it off Herman right before I shot his face off. I suspect they're coordinates."

Thompson walked over to a drawer and dug out a map. He then laid it out over the table and ran his fingers along the nodes, stopping once they hovered over the right spot. "Oh, yeah," he said. His finger honed in over the Brazilian rainforest. "Kline put our kill count at twenty-six. Ten alone were in Brazil." His finger tapped over different spots as he tallied, "Three here, four there, two more there, and who can forget the good *Herr* Fischer of Ushuaia."

Thompson snatched Herschel's flask just before it seasoned his lips. He took a pull and said, "That bag of gold teeth? Herman must have buried it years ago. The sale we thwarted was probably meant to facilitate his escape, and I bet these coordinates were his destination. This is where we need to go next."

"We'll never get clearance. Not after everything we just pulled," Vadim said.

"I told you, I'll handle Fink. Whatever the outcome is, we can't ignore this intel. We know Herman wasn't acting alone. Whoever else he was in contact with, I think we can safely assume these coordinates lead somewhere."

CHAPTER 6

TENSIONS RAN high by the sixth day. With no windows to distinguish between night and day, everyone's body clocks were out of whack. The only one consistently able to sleep was Herschel, who had been drowning in whiskey every single night. Initially, they found eight bottles in the safe house, and Herschel thus far had consumed three. On the seventh night, Thompson limited him to just eight ounces per day.

Nadir tried countless times to sleep. Each time she shut her eyes, her efforts were met with restless fidgeting. She resolved to prowl the attic in a netherworld state of sleepy animation.

Bar-Yochai and Vadim undertook an exercise regimen. Thompson finally put a stop to it when the entire attic began to stink of sweat. As team leader in a situation like this, it fell on him to play the motherly role.

Thompson did like to drink, but this was hardly the time or place. He limited his consumption to just three ounces per day. On the eighth night, he elected to take his ration back to back at 11:59 PM and 12:00 AM. It still didn't help him sleep. Insomnia had been his bane ever since he first saw combat. Even if he managed to doze, his dreams were always filled with flashbacks of gunfire, bloodshed, and screams.

On the ninth night, Thompson caught just a few winks of shuteye before a disturbance awoke him. Commotion sounded from beneath. When he recognized a voice speaking in muffled Russian, he muttered, "Fuck."

Breaking glass stirred the rest of Nesher Unit awake.

"Nobody panic," Thompson whispered. "I think the Soviets are searching below."

"I can grab the guns. I'm too light to creak the floorboards," Nadir offered.

"We won't need them," Thompson said. "Stay quiet and don't move a muscle."

Machine gun fire ensued after another loud bang. Everyone went stiff as a board. If the Soviets adjusted their weapons to the ceiling, it spelled the end of Nesher Unit.

The shots ended. Then laughter broke out. They listened as boots trailed all over the space beneath them.

"What are they doing?" Vadim whispered.

"Pigeonholing," answered Bar-Yochai. "They're probably checking every abandoned place in town."

"You sure picked a dogshit first field operation," Vadim whispered to Nadir.

"Shh!" Thompson hissed.

They continued listening. For all the rounds the men fired, it never occurred to them to direct their guns to the ceiling. It took an hour for the Soviets to give up and spew the place with a parting gift of lead.

Deafening silence ensued. "They won't be back," Thompson whispered. His lips pursed shut when additional gunfire drummed from below. A few bullets ripped through the floorboards and tore into the attic. Everyone remained on their beds with their hands covering their heads.

Only when a Soviet transport truck roared to life outside did they feel safe. "Is anyone hit?" Thompson asked.

"Negative," everyone morosely replied.

"Someone sure got smart at the end there," Vadim said.

"They'll check this place off the list after that," Thompson said. Beneath his iron confidence, even he harbored doubt. The men paid far more attention to the place than if they had merely been pigeonholing.

"This doesn't mean we can let our guard down," he added. "No more chatter unless necessary. Tip-toes only. If you're drinking, you're doing it in bed."

They spent the rest of their days walking on eggshells. At night, they rotated shifts to keep watch over the attic's trap door.

On the sixteenth night, Vadim took first watch. He didn't mind the task, for unlike the rest, he had much to occupy his downtime. His late father was an avid woodworker who taught him from an early age. Carving still served as a way to feel connected. He pulled out a small dreidel he'd been working on and set to work carving out a Gimel on its side.

To Vadim, there was something magical about the sound produced when a blade scraped against wood. The eerie silence of the attic amplified this feeling. His mind began to drift, first to the Budapest mission, then to the pain of losing Uzziel, and finally to his late father. He'd never forget his sister's shriek when she phoned to inform Vadim he'd suffered a fatal heart attack.

Vadim nearly had one himself. He dropped the dreidel when he heard commotion downstairs. He grabbed the Russian PPSh-41 submachine gun resting next to him and aimed at the trap door.

Two male voices were easily identifiable. How many more were beyond that, Vadim couldn't say. But he was about to find out, for the creak of the hidden entryway opening up signified that this time, the men knew what they were looking for.

Vadim considered firing through the floorboards. He might get lucky, and the sound would alert the rest of Nesher Unit. They'd be able to get the edge up and maybe even escape. Anything to avoid apprehension.

A single knock at the attic door gave Vadim cause for pause. He lowered the submachine gun and stared curiously.

"The sparrow flies high," said a voice in English.

The passcode, Vadim thought. He cleared all the heavy objects placed over the attic door, flipped the latch, and peeled it open. "But the eagle flies higher," he answered.

At the base of the ladder, three men dressed as Soviet soldiers looked up with great inconvenience. "Well come on, chaps! We haven't got all day," spoke one of the men with a British accent.

"Wait. Are you guys Brits?" Vadim asked.

"What could have possibly given it away?" the man mocked. "I'm Major Nigel Cummings, and these are my men, Yates Starkey, and Leslie Monday."

"Cheerio," Yates and Leslie said in unison, tipping their lambskin hats.

"We're MI-6," Nigel added. "Now go alert your team and let's get a move on. We've got a lot of ground to cover, and heaven knows I can't stand another second of this godforsaken Commie air."

"Two minutes," Vadim said. He stepped away to go wake everyone up.

They were all veterans at running on very little rest, and dismissing sleepiness came easy. But their departure hit a snag when it came to Uzziel. They wrapped him in a blanket but hadn't formed a solid plan to get him out.

Once Nigel saw the holdup, his face colored beat red. "Are you fucking with me?!" he exclaimed.

Thompson said, "I'm Thompson. I command this unit, and I can assure you, sir, I am not fucking with you. We're bringing our man home."

"The hell you are. I am not running a mortuary service behind enemy lines!" Nigel gaped.

"He's coming with, whether you like it not!"

"I don't believe this. We don't have time or room!"

"I am not laying one of my men to rest in a freezer! Either the body comes with, or you're going back empty-handed."

An eyebrow dance signaled Nigel's yield. "Help them," he told his two men.

They tied bedsheets together and used them to lower Uzziel's wrapped body down the trap door. Then they lugged the cadaver out back, where a large Soviet army truck waited to haul them all away.

"Quite the hike to retrieve you lot," said the driver as he put the truck in gear. "You must have cashed some serious favors to get us out here."

Thompson assumed the men from MI-6 had been minimally briefed at best. In all likelihood, they were told how many Americans to rescue and where, and nothing more.

The truck drove through alleyways as long as it could. When it turned onto the main road, they immediately encountered a Soviet blockade. A spotlight bathed the truck in blinding light.

"Well, that's not good," Vadim said. Thompson dealt him a death glare as Russian voices shouted at them from behind the spotlight.

"What are they saying?" Thompson asked.

"The jig is up. They're telling us to get out with our hands in the air," Nadir translated.

"Fat chance," Nigel said. The Brits were on assignment from the fearsome Colonel Stewart Schedule. Anyone to receive orders from Colonel Schedule executed them to the letter, without failure. One did not engage in any other alternative, lest they wished to maintain rank. Nigel would not be failing the Colonel, even if it cost him his life. He loaded a magazine into a Swiss Rexim Favor submachine gun and held it out the window.

"Wait!" Thompson said.

Nigel answered his plea with bullets. He blew out the spotlight and yelled "Go!" as returning fire raked the truck.

Everyone ducked and covered as bullets penetrated the cabin. The driver had them barreling away before anyone could suffer a hit.

"Hang tight. We're not out of this yet!" the driver called.

Sirens wailed to life from all over the city. The truck wasn't designed for speed, and to boot, it was grossly overloaded. Nigel glared at Thompson. He didn't need words to know it was over the added weight of their mortuary service.

The truck passed by a lone Soviet soldier. He fired eight shots at them and radioed their location.

"They're going to converge on us," Bar-Yochai announced.

"I hope you fellas have something faster than this big truck!" Vadim said.

"Make no mistake, chaps. We see our orders through," Nigel replied.

The driver came to a stop in the middle of an alley.

"Out we go," Nigel said.

"Bar, help me with Uzziel," Thompson said.

The two of them hoisted Uzziel out of the truck and followed. Nigel led them a few hundred paces ahead to a canal. Down in the water, there was a small boat chained to the canal wall.

"Drop your friend in. We don't have time to be graceful," Nigel said.

Thompson nodded for his soldiers to comply. They lowered Uzziel's wrapped body by the legs as far as they could reach before letting go. The body thudded in the boat without bouncing out.

One by one, the Brits and Nesher Unit scaled down the rope and into the boat. Nigel pulled the chain away, hit the engine, and hightailed it out of there. By the time the Soviets found the truck, Nesher Unit would be long gone.

CHAPTER 7

BAR-YOCHAI NEVER CARED for the sea. He considered it to be a mysterious and unholy place where men went to do two things-gather disgusting food or die horrible deaths. He'd shied away from marine life over his military career and secretly considered any high-seas affair to be a terrifying business. Heights? No problem. But even aboard a sizeable commercial freighter like the one they were on induced nauseating sickness.

"Forget your sea legs?" Vadim joked as Bar-Yochai clutched over a toilet bowl for the twentieth time.

"Never had 'em to begin with," he breathed between vomit heaves. "I hate the fucking ocean," he added. Then he blew chunks again. They had three more days to go in their already four-day-long voyage until they were back on dry land.

The MI-6 boys ferried Nesher Unit down the Danube River, to the connecting Drina River, all the way into the Adriatic Sea. There they boarded the British freighter bound for the U.K. They'd have nearly two weeks to strategize their next move before they'd fly stateside.

Uzziel's body began to smell early on the river voyage. By the time they reached the freighter, the stench had proved nauseating.

The MI-6 boys begrudgingly helped hoist the fetid corpse aboard the ship only if Thompson guaranteed they'd lay it to rest at sea immediately. The Captain seconded this notion strongly. Thompson grew angry when suggested they forgo a casket.

"My soldier gets a box, goddammit!" Thompson roared. They used wood from a few different crates to construct a casket big enough for Uzziel's body.

A storm brewed on the darkening horizon on the night they held Uzziel's funeral. Thompson read a brief but powerful eulogy on the ship deck and invited the rest of Nesher Unit to step up and say a few words. Seasoned soldiers shed tears of endless sorrow that night, something that stirred even the commercial crew. The men had no idea who their mysterious guests were. Even as strangers, they too felt remorseful.

Emotion plagued Nesher Unit for a few days after the funeral. It was like the safe house: Nobody spoke or did much of anything. Herschel drank, while Nadir passed the time in her cabin reading books and helping the seasick Bar-Yochai. Vadim chain-smoked and strolled the ship, his mind alight with silent contemplation. Nadir picked up the habit for herself thanks to an encounter with Vadim above deck.

Thompson found a set of golf clubs in a storage closet below deck. He knew he would have to report to a golf course for debriefing. It was how General Fink liked to weigh options- basked in sunlight and surrounded by green. He got two hours of practice hitting balls into the ocean. He could never hope to beat General Fink, but the closer the match, the better Thompson's odds were at getting what he wanted.

On the fifth day at sea, Thompson, Vadim, and Herschel had pent-up aggression to spend. They elected to let it off with a sparring matchup on the highest deck. Bar-Yochai's absence made for a queer playing field that felt unusually balanced.

Vadim fought Herschel in the first round. Herschel came in strong, throwing a succession of fast left-right jabs, but the nimble

Vadim slipped under his left arm and swept him to the ground. The two grappled all over the deck, grunting and swearing with each grasp of flesh.

The match came to an end when Vadim sprang free and threw a jump-spinning roundhouse kick. Herschel caught his leg midair, spun him like a merry-go-round and hurled him some fifteen feet away.

"Never leave the ground in a fight," Herschel lectured. "Once you do that, you're dead meat."

"Ouch," Vadim groaned as he peeled himself off the deck.

"You got anything left?" Herschel asked. He hardly even looked winded.

"Maybe later," Vadim said. He limped away to find a seat on a wooden crate. He then lit a cigarette and took a few deep puffs to nurse the pain.

"My turn," Thompson said. He'd learned to fight on the streets as a youth, but after enlisting, his martial arts capabilities had significantly expanded. He'd even learned a little Chinese Kung Fu. He struck a low stance that produced a broad smile from Herschel.

"You saw what happened to Vadim with the flashy kick, right?" he joked.

"He left the ground. Me? I know better," Thompson said.

They touched knuckles. Herschel started with a barrage of blindingly-fast punches, but Thompson easily countered and kicked him square in the ribs.

Unbeknownst to them, the commercial crew gambled over a winner. With one move, Thompson went from the underdog to the favorite.

Thompson faked Herschel from the left and came in from the right with a back fist. Herschel caught it. Thompson swore with surprise. Herschel took him down over his shoulder, but Thompson weaseled out of the hold and put Herschel in a lock of his own. Herschel went down hard. Before Thompson could get him in a choke, the captain of the ship interrupted:

"Whichever one of you goes by 'Eagle'," he called out. "You've got a radio call."

The two let go and straightened up. The organizer of the betting tried in vain to sneak away with everyone's cash. Vadim watched with particular amusement as the men surrounded him and forcibly retrieved their money.

The captain took Thompson below deck and excused himself for privacy. "This is Eagle," he spoke into the radio.

"Eagle, I have Birdman for you, sir," a voice replied.

"Put him through," Thompson said.

"Eagle," spoke General Fink in his hoarse voice. "Jesus H. Christ. Do you realize what I had to do to get you out?"

"We hit a snag, sir. We're just lucky you were able to pull whatever strings you did," Thompson replied.

Since the line wasn't secure, he'd save intimate details for the in-person briefing. "There's a lot to cover. We lost Raptor." Silence hung on the other end. "Are you there, sir?" he asked.

"I want a full debrief the instant you're on home soil. Until then, maintain radio silence. Over and out." The line went dead.

CHAPTER 8
THREE DAYS AGO - BRAZIL

"WHAT A GODFORSAKEN, MISERABLE HELLHOLE," Millbury groaned. His skin was a cocktail of sweat, dirt, mining chemicals, and unbeknownst to him, day-old Herpes-tainted blood from the excavator crushed to death from a falling tree. It missed Millbury by mere inches. Instead of washing off, Millbury just wiped his face with a dry towel and kept working. He considered the jungle's intense humidity to be a sufficient substitute. He was an unyielding Patlay worker, just the same as his father when he joined the company some sixty years prior.

Founded during the California Gold Rush, *Patlay Mining Company* had considerably expanded its operations over the last century, first across the country, then the world. Unbeknownst to shareholders, the company was also involved in numerous off-the-books expeditions just like this one. Only the most trusted workers were allowed to embark, and their pay reflected it. Patlay didn't even tell them what country they were being dispatched to, nor did it matter they had no legal right to be there. They'd strike riches and deal with whatever consequences later, just the same as they always did.

The site was hazardous, uncharted jungle. The tree density so daunted the first scouts that they elected to skip a ground effort and speculated from the air instead. The survey plane reported reserves of untold potential before mysteriously ceasing all radio contact. Patlay never bothered investigating the doomed plane's fate. Instead they covered it up and pressed ahead with the illicit expedition anyway. All of their covert operations were located in hostile climates that offered perilous, constant danger. Their very first off-shore operation to Africa in the 1920s proved to be such a disaster, Patlay had to hire an entirely new labor force of foreign contractors to stay on schedule. Of the ninety-two men who went, only thirteen returned. All thirteen penned resignation letters immediately thereafter.

Patlay learned from their mistakes. Instead of one giant, chaotic, underpaid workforce, now smaller, better-paid crews would go in for brief stages, segmenting the way for a more extensive operation down the road. In this case, only a dozen men were helicoptered in to start clearing the Brazilian site, and now one had already perished from a falling tree.

"Quit it with the AM boozing!" Millbury scolded one of his colleagues. The man shed a guilty look and tucked away his flask. Most of the men out there were raging alcoholics, something Millbury had little time for. He was the only one who considered himself a true professional. Saving the firewater for after dark wasn't just procedure, it might even save lives. Out here, a single drop of carelessness might cause the ultimate sacrifice. A replacement worker was at least a fortnight out, and they had already fallen behind schedule. If Millbury earned disdain from his colleagues as a slave driver, so be it. These were the sacrifices Patlay men made.

This was Millbury's third overseas expedition. He was pretty sure they were in Latin America, but where exactly was anyone's guess. He'd braved foreign tropics before and came out each time with a great sense of accomplished wisdom. Still, it always took a heavy psychological toll. The jungle did strange and cruel things to a person's mental state. Some found divinity, while others found madness. Millbury was no God-fearing Christian. He believed in the power of himself, and nothing more. He'd stared death in the face countless times, and each time, the reaper blinked.

When he went to take a piss, Millbury again found his hooded friend Death; this time it took the form of a black panther. The beast lowered its stance and growled. He removed his hand from his penis and reached for his knife. If the creature pounced, he'd drag it with him to hell.

The big cat growled and took a step forward. Millbury met the gesture with a curled lip. Though he knew the panther couldn't deduce meaning, he couldn't resist flexing. His urine stream ceased, but Millbury left his dick dangling as he stood frozen.

Suddenly a breaking branch spooked the creature to flee.

"What are you staring at?" an excavator asked when he found Millbury standing alone.

"Nothing. Trees are playing tricks on me, is all. Must be the heat. How's the north embankment coming?"

"There's a rock formation we didn't anticipate. Harrison is rigging the dynamite right now."

"Only use one stick. If we burn through our rations, we're fucked with a capital F," Millbury warned. On the home front, the workers used dynamite like water to combat any number of ailments. Out here, in limited quantities, rationing took priority.

Using a drill rigged to a generator, they inserted dynamite deep within the rock. They laid wires and then found safe cover.

A boom carried through the forest, sending birds near and far cawing into the air. The rock formation blew into pebbles that landed far from the blast site. A gaping crater now served as a new node in the excavation. But while the dynamite expelled most of the predators in the vicinity, it also beckoned unforeseen wrath.

The sight of white men alarmed them until they realized the trespassers were industrialists, not soldiers. They stalked from beyond the tree line, watching and waiting for the right moment to strike.

Shortly before nightfall, Millbury heard thunder in the distance. A quick soak or even a long one would be welcomed at this point.

Though he wasn't bathing, Millbury certainly couldn't complain if mother nature cared to intervene against his hygiene. He sat around the campfire and listened to a few stories before deciding to turn in.

Despite exhaustion, Millbury struggled to sleep. It took an hour of tossing and turning until he started to drift off. He didn't doze for long. A single gunshot forced his eyes open.

It's a dream, he thought. Then he heard a second gunshot. He grabbed his double-barrel shotgun and charged out of his tent.

A few more shots rang out in the darkness. All the Patlay excavators came armed to foreign expeditions. If the trouble were indigenous locals, the business end of his shotgun would out-power a bow and arrow no problem.

Millbury tip-toed around the campsite. Desolation greeted him everywhere he looked. A few spent shotgun shells littered the ground, along with an overturned soup bowl. Even the nighttime animals were quiet. His throat suddenly felt dry with fear. He swallowed to alleviate the burn and found the noise it generated carried louder than his footsteps. He didn't dare call anyone's name. He just crept around the site with his shotgun wedged against his shoulder.

He kept searching. When he saw a mass on the ground, he felt his heart rate skyrocket. "Hold it!" he boomed.

The mass remained silent. He crept up and turned it over to discover the body of another Patlay excavator. The man had a steel arrow bolt protruding from his chest.

Millbury turned away in revulsion. His eyes squinted to register a white hand holding a pistol right in his face. Who it belonged to, he would never know, for the pistol's point-blank flash was the last thing he ever saw.

CHAPTER 9

MI-6 TRAINED their personnel in a host of defensive and offensive tactics. At Fort Monckton, they learned advanced field tactics, hand-to-hand combat, and marksmanship. Two decades had elapsed since attending, and now Nigel considered he and his men expert soldiers. They always executed their orders, especially when they came from Colonel Schedule. Part of that meant no questions. Do the job. Get it done. On to the next.

But human curiosity remained. Nigel caught his men gossiping in their sleeping quarters. "They're Nazi hunters," Leslie said. "I'd bet five hundred quid on it."

"What makes you so sure?" Yates asked.

"For one, they're all Jews. Even the girl."

"Two of 'em, I'll give that to you. I'm not so sure about the rest. The one guy goes by Thompson. What kind of Jew name is that?"

"Names don't mean anything. They're well-trained Americans operating in a place nobody's got clearance for. The rescue order stemmed from the Colonel, so that means someone way high up is attached somewhere. I've heard rumors, Yates. These units exist. We don't have any because we weren't the ones who let half the high command slip away. I should buy 'em all drink to say thanks for the payback."

"You will do no such thing," Nigel scolded as he intruded into the room. "Pack your bags. We have new orders."

"But we're in the middle of the ocean," Yates complained.

"And it will likely be a very long, bumpy ride to shore. Now quit gossiping and gather all your things."

The men packed up in silence while Nigel ventured to Thompson's quarters. He found him sleeping peacefully with a newspaper covering his face.

Nigel considered waking him, but training dictated otherwise. Long goodbyes were reserved for civilians, not soldiers. He took his men's conversation into account and left a note that said, *"Happy hunting. Nigel"* next to his bed.

Nigel and his men gathered at the freighter's starboard side. A tiny single-engine skipper motored into view over the horizon to intercept the ship.

Nigel dispatched a rope ladder to the skipper and climbed down with his men.

On the ship deck, Herschel, Vadim, and Bar-Yochai emerged for fresh air. With his seasickness on the retreat, Bar-Yochai felt much improved. They watched the MI-6 boys disappear over the horizon.

"Let's get to it," Herschel said. Ever since the gambling riot caused by their sparring match, target practice and chess had been Nesher Unit's only actives to pass the time. Numerous crewmen approached Herschel and Vadim for a secret rematch in the cargo hold. Since the captain gifted them all a free lift, scorning his orders hindered on blasphemy.

Bar-Yochai tossed a few aluminum cans into the sea as Herschel prepped a Winchester Model 1895 rifle he borrowed from the crew.

"Five rounds," Bar-Yochai announced. "Only counts if you sink the can."

Vadim watched the cans floating in the distance from his binoculars. "Go," he said.

Herschel fired two shots.

"Hit. Hit," Vadim said, keeping the binoculars pinned to his eyes.

Herschel fired a third shot and waited.

"Hit," Vadim said.

Herschel earned his title "The Hammer" during Operation Varsity when he air-dropped off-course into a hostile German city and had to fight his way out single-handedly. Over the course of three days, he racked up a kill count that rivaled that of a mythic Greek god. He was a first-draft pick for Thompson during Nesher Unit's formation.

After two more shots, Herschel lowered his rifle. "You missed the last one," Vadim said.

"Look again," Herschel replied, tossing Bar-Yochai the rifle.

"Hmm. I stand corrected. It's going down."

Herschel fished out a cigarette and stuck it in his lips. He didn't have time to light it. Bar-Yochai ripped off five quick shots without any pause.

"All hits," Vadim said.

A Brooklyn-raised Jew, Bar-Yochai had known Thompson since their Hebrew School days. Bar-Yochai was seven years Thompson's senior and now the oldest member of Nesher Unit at the age of 44. While Thompson had always been the careful, strategic type, Bar-Yochai was all bullets and brawn. Their military career together reflected it- the only difference being both men were equally skilled with a firearm, second only to Uzziel. With him gone, the team's top marksman would remain contested.

Bar-Yochai lowered the gun and handed it to Vadim. He looked it over and said, "You know what? You've made me lose all taste. How about a drinking game instead?"

"Giving up already?" Nadir asked.

"Oh, look who it is. Read every book on the ship, have you?" Vadim teased.

"Twice, now. I need something more spirited. Give me the gun."

Vadim shrugged and handed Nadir the rifle. She checked it over, cocked it, and aimed.

"Now when you pull the trigger, don't-"

Vadim's explanation curtailed as Nadir fired five shots almost as fast as Bar-Yochai. He wordlessly lifted the binoculars and said, "Four hits. One miss."

Nadir made a sour face, loaded a new magazine, retrained the rifle, and fired another shot. "Hit," Vadim said.

"Let's be clear. I haven't been in the field because I like supporting from afar, not because I can't shoot," Nadir clarified.

Their gunfire eventually stirred Thompson in his sleeping quarters. He ventured above deck to find his crew standing amidst a pile of spent shell casings.

"I think you kids have had enough," Thompson said. "I passed the captain on the way up here. Judging by the look on his face, I'd say we're fast wearing out our welcome. I have the social quarters reserved for an hour. What do you say we all go down for a little chat?"

Once everyone took a seat below deck, Thompson began, "I have no idea what's going to happen once we get back. For argument's sake, let's assume we aren't shut down. We have a big choice to make regarding our next move. The more I think about it, the more I think Jinter Boozis is our best clue at crossing the rest of the names off our list."

Nadir folded her arms. "We can't go back into Soviet Territory. Not yet, anyway" she said. "If Jinter had any family or friends hiding behind red lines, for the time being, they remain untouchable."

"Let's talk about the facts," Herschel said. "Soviet territory might be too hot, but South America is a different story. We've never left so much as a footprint in all our Brazilian operations. We know for certain Kline was in contact with Hermann Michael as recently as two months ago. Where Jinter Boozis entered the picture is anyone's guess, but suddenly Herman comes out of hiding to do some risky business. I don't think that scrap of paper was just a pair of random numbers. Those were coordinates. I bet if we go there, we'll find a few names."

"I want everyone on the same page. Vadim? Bar? Nadir? What are your thoughts?" Thompson asked.

"No doubt, Brazil should be our next target," Nadir said. "But there's a big problem. These coordinates look like the deep jungle. How are we going to get there without being detected? There are probably just a few roads if that."

"I might have a few ideas," replied Thompson.

"Like what?"

Thompson smiled. "Well for starters, who said anything about going by land?"

CHAPTER 10

They arrived in England at dawn, stepping off the freighter to encounter two men sporting suits and bowler hats. Thompson figured them for MI-6 and let his guess suffice, for they did not exchange a word. The men stuffed Nesher Unit into a pair of government-issued Land Rovers sped them across the English countryside as if their very presence fouled the landscape. The Land Rovers tore into an airfield and came to a break-neck stop right at the entrance ramp of a Fairchild C-123 Provider. Its propellers were already spinning in anticipation of a hasty departure.

"Kind of a passive-aggressive bunch here, no?" Vadim said to Herschel.

"I think they're mad. We've inconvenienced them, and they've all been told not to even look at us."

"They're just bored. They wish they saw action like us. Especially the guy who drove us."

Severe turbulence rocked the return flight to Hanscom Air Force Base. Bar-Yochai, still bearing pale complexion from his seasickness, figured he'd lost at least ten pounds. At a particularly rough patch during the flight, he braced for yet another vomiting spell. But there was nothing left in his stomach to upchuck, and all he could do was dry heave.

━━━

Nearly seven weeks after departing the U.S., Nesher Unit touched down in Maryland. A uniformed Army Major awaited their arrival on the tarmac with a sealed envelope in his hand. The Major saluted Thompson when he stepped off the plane and handed him the envelope.

Everyone gathered around Thompson as he slit it open with a knife. The letter, stamped "TOP SECRET," read:

"ORDERS:

THOMPSON: REPORT TO TEXAS FOR DEBRIEF. MAJOR WILL PROVIDE TRANSPORT.

UNIT: LEAVE OF ABSENCE UNTIL FURTHER NOTICE."

"I guess you're all on vacation for a while," Thompson announced."

"Who's to say we don't take a little R and R in Texas? It's a small world, you know, and I could use some warm sun," Bar-Yochai suggested.

"I don't want to pull Fink's tail like that. Whatever he has to say, he probably made up his mind a week ago. Your presence in Texas would only annoy him."

"He wouldn't know."

"The hell he wouldn't. He's a reasonable man, Bar. He'll see the mission for what it was."

"And if he doesn't?" Bar-Yochai asked.

"Then it's been a pleasure serving as your commanding officer. Unit dismissed."

"Yes, sir!" everyone replied, saluting Thompson. He returned the gesture and then followed the Major into an olive-green army jeep. The Major shuttled him straight across the airfield and stuck him aboard a Convair C-131 Samaritan bound for Texas.

G eneral Alan Rochester Fink was the eldest son of a Los Angeles Orthodox Jewish family. In 1917, he turned renegade to tradition by enlisting to fight in World War I. He returned home battered, hardened, and convinced divine intervention saved him. Much to his dismay, his tale was greeted with doubt from his father, who outcast him for forsaking the Orthodox Jewish way. He interpreted it as a sign to return to the service, to save the lives of others and reign superiority in the name of God and the United States.

When the world returned to war for the second time, Fink rose to the rank of General with brutal and clever tactics that cast fear into the hearts of Hitler's henchmen. He considered the Jewish extermination to be a personal insult, and the United States war machine became the ultimate tool for Fink's vendetta. He hatched several risky operations to capture or kill high-ranking Nazis, earning him the nickname "Hitler's Hangman." But his quest for vengeance wouldn't be stopped at Nuremberg. Too many Nazis escaped justice for Fink's liking, and using his influence, he founded Nesher Unit as a top-secret pet project. Nesher was Fink's rabid dog, and whenever it caught a rabbit, the pack leader, Thompson, reported to his master. Never once had it been outside of a golf course.

Thompson didn't much care for the sport. However, there was something distinctly satisfying about the sound a driver produced when it clanged against a ball. It became a tiny white dot against the crisp blue sky, arching wide to overcut the course and land perfectly in line for an Eagle.

"Hot damn! Now that's how you drive a ball," General Fink boasted. "I almost forgot I'm furious with you," he added, taking a drag of his cigar as he started off with his clubs. A stern believer in working for oneself, Fink never employed a caddie. He found his ball and hit it perfectly to best Thompson's shot.

"Maybe you can convince Stalin to settle things over eighteen holes," Thompson said to divert the subject.

"Knowing a Soviet, I'm sure he'd say 'Da' and then set the match somewhere in Siberia," General Fink said. "Plus, there's no money in easing tensions. In case you didn't get the memo from Washington, it's all about dollars and cents now, Avery. Somewhere over the last eight years, top brass got it in their heads warfare's a great business opportunity. I don't see any cents in it, if you ask me, though."

Thompson tried not to roll his eyes at Fink's pun as they walked to their balls. "Well, if you ask me, sir, building a warfare enterprise is exactly the kind of thinking that destroys nations."

Thompson took a few practice swings at his ball and continued, "I'd say it's how Hitler saw things, and look how that turned out. Re-armament is precisely what jumpstarted the German economy." He swung. The ball sliced to the right and obliterated any hopes he had at an Eagle.

"You'll recover for a par," patronized General Fink.

"Maybe, but I'll need better than par to beat you, sir," Thompson said.

"Rules of warfare, Avery- know thy enemy. You should have abandoned any hope of victory before setting foot on the green with me," General Fink said. "Now, speaking of grilled meat, enough shooting the shit."

General Fink dropped his clubs and put his hands to his hips. Thompson regarded him with particular infamy for how quickly he switched gears. "They were swarming like a nest of angry hornets in Budapest. We had to clear out every single deep cover operative because of the mess you caused. Tell me what the good fuck happened?!"

"We tracked Herman Kline to the black-market merchant, Jinter Boozis, but the streets were too crowded to make a move. Uzziel was standing in the window of an apartment across the street for supporting fire. When we went into the merchant's store, everything went to hell. Herman fled out the back after shooting at us. Uzziel clipped him once, but his gun jammed. Herman stole a car. Bar-Yochai and I pursued, found him, and put a dozen bullets in his face."

"And your man Uzziel?"

"Apprehended leaving the scene. Soviets drew guns. He drew back and took a slug to the gut. We were able to get him out of there, but there was nothing we could do to save him."

"I see," General Fink said.

"It's bad, sir- I know- but it couldn't be helped. Herman wasn't going down without a fight. I'm positive we left him unidentifiable. And the jewelry store burned down too, so there was little evidence left. The Soviets know we were foreign, but we could have been anyone. Our guns were Russian, and our faces were mostly unseen."

"That doesn't excuse the fact you were almost caught. Do you know what that could mean for global relations if an American hit-squad was captured on a secret operation tearing up a Soviet satellite state?"

"We weren't though."

General Fink stared dubiously. "I had to burn my only MI-6 favor to get you out."

"I assure you, it was necessary, sir." Thompson picked up General Fink's clubs and handed them over.

General Fink took the bag. "Against my better judgment, I'm not disbanding you. Not yet anyway. Do you have a replacement in mind for Uzziel?"

They started walking again. "No," Thompson flatly said. He decided on the freighter the bond he felt with his comrades was unbreakable, even in death. Replacing a link to such a well-forged chain seemed inconceivable. "It wouldn't be good for the team. Not yet, at least."

"Very well. I'll leave that to your discretion." General Fink tossed his finished cigar away and immediately lit another. Then he took a long, slow drag. "You know back when I was in the trenches in France, and we had this guy. Private First-Class Don Eisman, the company comedian. Even as chlorine clouds rolled through those trenches, he was the one who kept us grinning behind those godforsaken gas masks. Nothing could phase this guy. Then one day, it's a shit storm. Germans pouring in all around us, and we're fighting like dogs. Eisman got a rat in his boot that bit him in the toe. He died of infection two days later. All that danger, and the way he fearlessly faced it, and in the end, a fucking rat is what got him." He took a few more drags and added, "I trust you see the virtue?"

"Shit happens," murmured Thompson as he swung. The flash of Uzziel dying in the bed blared through his mind and muddied his aim. The ball zinged out of the bunker and bounced off a tree.

"Don't beat yourself up, Avery. Your people know what they signed up for. You lost a man, but you nabbed a monster to our people. I bet Uzziel would gladly die again for it. Remember that."

"I know it wasn't for nothing, sir. But Herman was just the tip of the iceberg," Thompson said. General Fink stared probingly. "Since you said Washington is all business, what I am going to ask you for next is a high-risk, high-return scenario."

"Oh?"

"We had a few minutes to interrogate Herman. He didn't give anything up, but we did manage to find this in his pocket." Thompson handed General Fink the piece of paper they collected from Herman.

"What are these?" General Fink asked.

"The key, maybe. Herman had a bag of gold teeth he was trying to sell for- we believe- safe passage somewhere. Jinter Boozis died in the shootout, but whatever his Nazi ties were, we're certain he was helping other fugitives. We think these coordinates were where he was sending Herman. It's in the remote jungles of Brazil."

"Just so I'm clear here... You've come to this debriefing where one of your men was killed, and an international incident narrowly avoided, all to ask for *another* high-risk operation?"

"No risk, no reward. Simple business economics, as you said."

General Fink looked stumped. He took a few more puffs and

stared up at the sky. "Jesus," he said, shaking his head. "You really are a head case. You know that?"

"Sir, you can't deny our successes in South America. It's as you said when you formed Nesher Unit- These Nazi fugitives pose a continued threat to national security. If we don't leap on this right now, it could bite the whole nation in the ass down the line."

"Even if I was on board with this, after what just happened in Budapest-"

"Sir, with all due respect, do I really need to spell this out? What if a dozen fugitives are living together, or more? Who knows what they might be planning? It's already been weeks since we took out Kline. How long until these guys realize they might be compromised?"

General Fink still shook his head. "I had to move heaven and earth to keep Budapest off the President's desk. This isn't just your career, Thompson. It's all of ours. In case you forgot, that whole region is just as much of a diplomatic nightmare as eastern Europe is. If you're apprehended, it won't just be the end of Nesher Unit."

"It's dense jungle, and if we take down ten men with one operation, it saves us years."

"If... Even if I agreed to this, how the hell would you get there? I'm not deploying your unit from another hostile city where you might be spotted."

"We've got it all worked out, sir. I just need your approval."

General Fink suspiciously said as he put the cigar back to his lips, "Let's hear it."

"I assume you're familiar with the *Devil's Brigade*, sir?" Thompson said.

"The Canadian/American airborne ranger unit, right? Little joint-nation exercise, kind of like how we do things with Israel," General Fink said.

"That's right. Herschel did a drop with them back in '44. One of their guys might be willing to give us a crash course. We'll drop in from the air and execute a five-day sweep. We get in, take a look around, and we get out. Nobody knows we were ever even there. If we find something, great. If not, at least we looked."

"What about extraction? We can't send a chopper. We can't land a plane. There are no roads to speak of either."

"A little while back I saw Central Intelligence was working on a new type of miniature submersible- something small enough to navigate down a river. If you have any left, sir, cash a favor and see if they'll send a crew to get us out."

General Fink pondered. "This has to be an airtight, barebones plan. No radios or anything else that could be intercepted. Small arms only. Call it an exploratory walk through the trees, at best. Can your people handle something so extreme?"

"You better believe it, sir," Thompson replied.

"You talk the talk, Avery. I'll give you that," General Fink came upon his golf ball and lined up for his shot. He smacked the ball and watched it fly through the air. It landed mere inches from the hole.

"Alright," he conceded. "I'll make some calls. But your team better be well-prepared. I want to see more than a crash course in air dropping. If anything goes awry, it's entirely on you."

"Understood," Thompson said. He wasn't just staking Nesher Unit on this. This meant entire careers.

CHAPTER 11

No MATTER how many years elapsed, Nadir remained haunted by hellish memories forever engrained in her mind. Every time she shut her eyes at night, her cruel subconscious forced her to relive events:

Before Hitler, the Horowitz family prospered owning a grocery store in Munich. But then came the first anti-Jewish laws, followed by an eerie calm that shattered during *Kristallnacht*. Suddenly the Horowitz's were just another family swept into the ghettos. They would spend almost a year there until the final purge to the camps.

It was a Friday afternoon when Nadir stepped out for a short walk. She returned just in time to see both of her parents thrown in front of a wall and shot. What became of her brother and sister, she would never know, for the ensuing hours were pure chaos as everyone was rounded up and stuffed aboard cattle cars. She slipped away amidst the fervor and found a hidden crawl space in an apartment boiler room, where she remained for six days. After the last troops swept through, she found a tiny hole in the ghetto wall and fled south.

How Nadir managed to hide for four more years was nothing short of miraculous. She learned to be stealthy, cunning, and even to kill. Two weeks on the run, in a dark alley, a lone soldier accosted her for "looking Jewish." She drew him close by showing him her bare breasts, only to cut his throat the instant he dropped his guard.

Her exodus from the cities took almost two months and claimed the lives of three more Nazis. She made her way further south, hopping from farm to farm and traveling only under cover of darkness.

Thirty-four months elapsed until she came across a farm tilled by a senile deaf old man. She hid there for ten months until Uzziel and his unit swept through in late 1944. When she spotted them, she panicked and hid under a pile of hay. But it wasn't German the men spoke. It was *English*. When she popped up from the hay, Uzziel nearly shot her. Then he realized who he was looking at: a starving fellow-tribesman; *A Jewish girl!* He threw his gun aside and scooped her up in his arms.

Uzziel stayed with Nadir as she recovered with his unit. She spoke fluent English, Hebrew, and even a little Russian. Once she returned to health, Uzziel got her out of Europe and set her up at her uncle Rafa's house in Chicago. She'd never met Rafa until the night she turned up on his doorstep, but he welcomed her as if she'd lived there her whole life.

Uzziel argued Nadir helped the war effort with her kills and petitioned to make her an American. With her citizenship affirmed, she attempted to enlist in late 1945. The army denied her.

Uzziel wouldn't have it. On her second attempt, armed with Uzziel's letter of recommendation, the army accepted Nadir as an intelligence recruit. It was a charity position, honored only out of respect for Uzziel, but shortly after admittance, she left her superiors mystified.

In three short years, Nadir earned five promotions. She left her post when Thompson recruited her one crisp January morning in 1950. He'd heard rumors, and after drafting Uzziel as his long-range gunner, she seemed like an obvious pick for intelligence chief. Every good predator needed a keen set of eyes, and with the name *Nesher* being Hebrew for "Eagle," there was no emphasis lost on Nadir's significance.

———

It was the dead of night when the government-commissioned Chevy 210 dropped Nadir off at Rafa's Chicago residence- a two-story home on the south side. She liked to turn up unannounced at his little red house, and she left just the same. Rafa hated long goodbyes and took no offense when she'd vanish and reappear, sometimes days, other times months later. He found her sitting in his kitchen smoking a cigarette in the dark.

"Either you're a very lazy burglar, or a terrible house guest, Nadir. Put that thing out," Rafa scolded. He flipped on the light to confirm his niece.

"They're your cigarettes," Nadir answered.

"And you may help yourself, child, but not in the damn kitchen! I just had these walls painted!" He relaxed his expression and looked her up and down. "*Oy, yoi, yoi!* More muscle on this girl than most of the construction workers I see on Third Street." He came forward and kissed her on the cheek. "Can I make you something to eat?"

"It's late. The cigarette is fine. I wasn't planning to wake you."

Rafa took a seat at the kitchen table and lit a cigarette of his own. When she shot him a dirty look, he fired back, "My house, my rules. I can smoke in here. You? Well, you make me proud. Just not *that* proud. If you can become the first female four-star general, maybe you'll get cigarette privileges," he teased.

"How about three stars?"

"We'll call it an even two," Rafa said, ashing. "You were gone for quite a while this time."

Nadir took a deep drag and put it out. She diverted her gaze away to hide a tear blossoming in the corner of her eye.

"Oh, no. What's wrong?"

She wiped the tear from her eye and said, "Sorry."

"Never apologize for being human, unless you're an asshole," Rafa said. Nadir laughed and hugged him.

"Thank you. We..." Nadir sighed, annoyed she leaked emotion as she tried to keep herself together. "Uzziel got killed, Rafa!" The words, uttering them so matter-of-factly, stabbed her emotions in a way she hadn't yet felt. She fought with all her might to remain calm. "It's okay," she affirmed aloud, more to tell herself a falsehood to ease her weeping.

"I know you can't tell me details, but-"

"A police officer shot him," Nadir blurted, "A foreign one. In the stomach. It wasn't clean. It wasn't decent. It wasn't how a man like that should have died." She paused a wiped away another tear. "Shit. I shouldn't have said any of that. Forget what you just heard, Rafa. I'm sorry."

Rafa laid his hand on Nadir's and said, "Like my rabbi once said to me on the *bema* when I was a boy, 'Rafa, you're a young man of many secrets, and it is my hope, in time, you will share them with me. But it's up to you to do that, whenever you're ready.'"

He took another drag and said, "Honestly, I always thought it was a very strange thing to say to a young person, and still do, but in this case, forget the *chazzer*, think of the quote. You're a strong girl. Nobody knows it better than you, Nadir. I think, if anything, Uzziel would only want you to carry forward."

He offered her a second cigarette and said, "I'll assume you made General somewhere over these past few months and are just being modest."

Nadir lit the cigarette. The pain in her lungs became less intense, as were the buzzes. She'd never been a smoker, but ever since the freighter, she'd burned through at least a dozen packs. Her mounting stress felt inhuman. She needed something to subtract the edge, and she hated drunks.

"Will you be here longer than a few days, you think?" Rafa asked. A seasoned smoker, in five short puffs, half of his cigarette vanquished to ash.

"I can't say. Not because it's classified. I really don't know. If it were up to me, we'd already be on our way somewhere else. Thompson's finding out now. It could be days or even months."

Nadir put out her cigarette and kissed Rafa on the cheek. "I'm going to bed. In the morning, after I train for a bit, let's get breakfast. My treat."

"Goodnight, General," Rafa said. He put out the Lucky Strike as it neared burning his fingers. Then he fished another out of his pack and drew a match.

Everything in Nadir's bedroom looked just as she'd left it. In all likelihood, Rafa hadn't once set foot inside. He always respected her privacy, even in her absence.

She opened her dresser and found an old photograph of her parents. She never brought it with on missions and seeing it after such a perilous ordeal brought comfort. Not enough, though, for she only caught a few hours of sleep that night.

At dawn, she dressed and went for a long run to weight her options. If Nesher Unit disbanded, she might retire from the military for good.

But then what?

Perhaps she'd open a grocery store like her late father? Or maybe she could storm the male-driven world of business and stake her claim there?

The only conclusion she reached by the end of the run was nothing could bring solace if her life's greatest chapter came to such an abrupt and unsavory end.

Nadir showered and then went to breakfast at a diner with Rafa. "Whatever comes next, you have to keep one thing in mind," he said. "You're too young to worry, child. Take it from an old man- nothing puts lines on your face like stress."

He took a sip of coffee and said, "Do you know why I left the old country in the first place?"

"Because your store got destroyed in the first world war?" Nadir said.

"Partly. I didn't see how I could rebuild. Not after losing it all. And do you know what? I'm thriving in my old age because of it. If I'd never endured that tragedy, we wouldn't be sitting here enjoying this meal. You're too worried about something that's out of your hands, Nadir. Didn't you learn anything in school? God has a plan for us all. It may not seem fair, and it may not make sense, but in time, I promise it will."

Nadir rolled her eyes. "You aren't the first to try and sell me on that," she said.

"Think what you want, my dear. But whatever happens next, I don't have a doubt in my mind you'll land on your feet."

A week fell off the clock, and nothing could calm Nadir's nerves. The coordinates presented a window of opportunity that was shrinking by the day. She stirred awake, pacing around on very little sleep for days on end. When she wasn't exercising, she was chain smoking. It all proved futile, for until she knew Nesher Unit's fate, uncertainty reigned supreme over her mindset.

On the seventh night, she awoke in the midst a thunderstorm. She peeled herself off the sweaty ice-cold sheets and made her way down to the kitchen. She rummaged through the cupboard, where she found the old Browning M1900 pistol that Rafa kept. She laid it on the table and disassembled it for cleaning. Rafa stumbled upon her halfway through the task.

"It hasn't moved since you last cleaned it, you know," Rafa said.

"I can tell. I just like all the pieces laid out like this. It gives me a sense of control. Don't ask how or why."

Rafa looked at her strangely.

"If nothing else, it's an antique," she added. "When was the last time you discharged it?"

"Never," Rafa said. "I don't even know how to load it."

"Then why do you keep it? It's worth money, Rafa."

"That pistol you're holding belonged to my father. He bought it in the old country at the turn of the century and gave it to me when I was leaving for America. He thought this place was dangerous and said I should have it. Gets me every time I think about it."

"My father used to have a gun just like this. It didn't keep anyone safe."

"That's because you weren't the one holding it. Don't forget. A weapon is nothing without its wielder," he said. "Keep it. Just make sure it gets some use."

Every member of Nesher Unit had a favorite sidearm they brought with on most missions. Thompson and Herschel had Colt 1911s; Vadim with his Smith and Wesson .38 snub nose; and Bar-Yochai with his Beretta M1951. If Nesher Unit survived, Nadir would finally be as battle-ready as her compatriots.

Nadir ventured to the cupboard to see how many bullets Rafa had stored away. She only counted out a few before a loud knock interrupted her. A jolt stabbed through her stomach, for just one person could be turning up at her doorstep in the middle of the night.

"Nadir," called Rafa. "You've got company."

Nadir stepped into the front entryway. Thompson and Vadim were dripping wet. Rafa excused himself to give them privacy.

"Sorry to leave you in the dark for a week. I figured I'd tell you the word in person," Thompson said.

Nadir bore a grim face. "News so bad, you forgot your umbrellas?" she asked.

"Hardly. We're just getting acclimated is all," Vadim said.

"Acclimated?" Nadir asked.

"Yeah, I hear it rains ten times a day where we're going."

Nadir opened her mouth to speak, but excitement tripped her tongue. "You mean we're not shut down?!"

Thompson shook his head. "Make no mistake, we're on thin ice, but we've got clearance. There's a plane waiting for us at Chanute. Anything you need, go get it now."

"Ready to roll," Nadir replied as she showed them the fully-assembled Browning. "Let's not waste another second."

CHAPTER 12

KOHN MEN BECAME doctors for as far back as the family could trace its lineage. Two days before the Japanese struck Pearl Harbor, Vadim Kohn received word he'd been admitted to Harvard Medical School. He was to be the fifth legacy until he learned a childhood friend had been killed in the attack. It left a sordid taste in his mouth, one he knew wouldn't subside until he served his country.

Vadim braved frigid temperatures in a block-long line on December 8th to enlist as an Army medic. He served fearlessly in the Pacific theater, saving lives, and taking them, too. In early 1945, he was captured and made prisoner in the Philippians. On a nightmarish death-march through the hills, he slipped a jagged rock in the grip of his toes. Then under cover of darkness, he used it to saw through his bamboo cage, escaped, and lead a battalion back two days later to liberate the camp. He never saw himself as a soldier before the war, but after the guns fell silent, he couldn't imagine any other way to live.

Vadim remained in the service, much to his family's dismay. He officially earned his medical doctorate while instructing newly-enlisted medics at Fort Benning, Georgia. He bounced around from base to base, performing medical seminars and making a reputation for his cheeky humor. It earned him a spot on Nesher Unit's draft list for field medics. "Hunting some Germans, and you want me to tag along?" Vadim said with a laugh when Thompson approached him in a bar off base. "Never got to shoot a Jerry, you know. Sign me up." Since then, Thompson found Vadim less and less humorous. A sibling-like bond developed between the two which frequently bloomed quarrel.

━━

"Would you pull it together?" Thompson nagged. "We haven't even gotten to the snakes yet." He knew Vadim hated two things in life- heights and snakes. Thompson hadn't a doubt in his mind Vadim would never forget this day, and it was only just beginning.

Even Nesher Unit's training missions had to be covered up. Their exercise in the Florida Everglades was dubbed as a prototype test for a new T-10 Parachute. When told his life would be in the hands of a prototype, Vadim nearly vomited his lunch on the spot. Even after two days of on-the-ground training and three practice jumps over Fort Benning, he still lacked any form of confidence. He tried to hide his trembling hands as the rear cargo doors of the rickety Douglas C-133 Cargomaster peeled open to evacuate all the air.

"This one's going to blow chunks like a volcano!" Jacks yelled with a laugh. Despite the intense wind, Vadim smelled traces of whiskey on his breath. The Canadian airborne-ranger veteran put on an animated crash course for Nesher Unit. Thompson, Herschel, and Bar-Yochai had all airdropped in the past, but for Vadim and Nadir, the information was new. And unlike Vadim, Nadir eagerly looked down at the puffy clouds as she slid her goggles over her eyes.

"Hey," Jacks yelled, grabbing Vadim's shoulder and slapping him across the face, "I didn't spend two days educating you lot to jump out and die on me. You've already done it three times, Kohn! Why so nervous? Look at those clouds out there! Who else gets to play God like this? You're too handsome to wind up as gator food."

"You sure have a magical way of encouragement, Jacks," Vadim told the *Devil's Brigade* man. He slid his goggles over his eyes and shook his head, muttering, "Here goes nothing."

"Positions," Jacks shouted. He wanted to tag along, but Thompson felt his presence would be an intrusion. He was still considering Uzziel's replacement. A loud-mouth, drunken *goy* certainly didn't fit the bill.

Thompson lined up first. He called back, "Just like we practiced," and dropped out of the plane.

Bar-Yochai yelled, "Last pair of boots on the ground is buying drinks when we're back," and jumped out after Thompson.

Herschel shrugged and quietly followed suit.

Nadir looked at Vadim and said, "Ready?"

"Not really," he nervously replied. "You know, when I signed up for this, Thompson never-"

"Relax!" Jacks yelled, shoving Vadim out of the plane. His screams quickly trailed off as he plummeted to the earth.

Nadir gaped at Jacks. "Are you crazy?!" she yelled.

"Go catch him," Jacks suggested.

Nadir scowled at Jacks and dove arms first after Vadim.

Jacks whistled in amazement as his eyes tracked her descent. "She's a natural if I've ever seen one," he remarked to himself as he closed the cargo doors.

Nadir tore through the sky like a falcon and found Vadim help-lessly flailing and screaming bloody murder. She caught him by the wrist and pulled him close. "Quit panicking!" he thought he heard Nadir yell. Or maybe it was, "You're a man, Vadim!" Whatever she said, he just wanted the whole thing to be over with.

Blinding moisture buffeted them as they hit the clouds. Vadim couldn't see anything beyond Nadir's hand, which remained tightly gripped around his wrist. She pulled him close to reveal an ecstatic smile. She tried to yell something, but so much air rushed into her mouth all she could do was grin.

Nadir's whole body came into illumination for Vadim as they tumbled through the cloud ceiling to look down on a sea of green. The air turned from ice-cold to muggy hot as the Everglades beneath grew wide. Nadir signaled her ripcord and mouthed, "NOW."

She let go of Vadim and pulled her ripcord to expel the T-10 Parachute. The nylon material made a loud crack when it expanded. She looked for Vadim. He'd disappeared.

Vadim's heart skipped a beat as he fruitlessly pulled the ripcord. He knew it spelled certain doom when he could distinctly make out the details of all the trees. The T-10 Parachute was designed for a 500-foot minimum deployment. This prototype boasted 400 feet. It would be a real test, for he had milliseconds until breaching the threshold. He yanked the backup cord and felt his body jolt with force upon the parachute's deployment.

The chute couldn't begin stopping power until 250 feet. A doctor like Vadim knew two broken legs when he saw them, and that was his best-case scenario, he thought at 100 feet. He screamed as he plunged through the trees like a cannon-ball, branches snapping and raking his whole body.

Vadim hung six feet up, his chute having snagged on a branch. "Jesus. Fucking. Christ," he breathed. He sat in silence for a few seconds and then screamed, "I have to do that again?!" Birds cawed in disturbance and flew away.

"What happened?" a voice called. Vadim looked down to see Thompson, Bar-Yochai, and Herschel standing underneath.

"This piece-of-shit nearly got me killed!" Vadim roared. He took out a knife and started sawing himself free.

"Keep your voice down. It's a training exercise," Thompson reminded. Vadim restrained his urge to snap back.

"I'd like to point out Vadim has yet to touch the ground," Herschel said. "That means there's a double pour of aged scotch with my name on it."

Vadim growled in frustration. "Shove it up your ass, Herschel. I'd gladly take another month in that Jap-camp over dropping like that again," he yelled.

"Vadim, did you soil yourself?" Herschel asked. He turned to everyone else and said, "I think he's embarrassed is all, fellas."

"Are you alright?" Nadir called up. Vadim stopped to see she made it safely to the ground.

"I've been better, thanks," Vadim replied. "Looked like you had plenty of fun, though."

Thompson commanded a hardened brigade. Petrified or not, Vadim's tone sounded anything but. "If you want off this mission, now is the time."

"Don't kid yourself, Avery. You'd be dead meat without me. No, sir. I'll do another sky dance if it means one less Kraut. I don't have to enjoy it, but I'll sure as shit do it," he said.

He put the knife away with his free hand and said, "Heads up," before dropping down. He had no less than thirty new cuts and scratches on his face and hands. His uniform was torn, and blood ran freely down his face mixing with dirt and sap from the leaves.

"You didn't break anything, did you?" Thompson asked.

"Just my pride. Where to?" Vadim replied, dusting himself off.

Thompson laid out a map on the soil. "We're in the driest patch of the Everglades. There's more swamp in this terrain than what we'll encounter in Brazil, but the climate will be similar. Today and tomorrow are about endurance. Fink made it abundantly clear we're all alone this time. That means no mistakes. I need to confirm we all have the stamina, so we've got a twenty-click hike ahead of us before we make camp. Keep chatter to a minimum. We don't know what we're going to find in the field, so let's not develop any bad habits here," Thompson said, looking at Vadim.

"I cashed in my one outburst. There won't be a second."

"You've already made a fatal mistake, though," Thompson said, folding up the map.

"And what's that?"

Thompson pointed up the tree. Vadim's ragged parachute still hung from the branches.

"It's the Everglades. Nobody's going to find it," Vadim reasoned.

"In the field, a mistake like that could cost everything," Thompson said.

"Would you like me to climb up and get it?" Vadim asked.

"Leave it. Just don't forget it next time. Let's get a move on," Thompson said. He took out a machete and started cutting a path through the brush.

"Not a trace, huh?" Vadim teased, pointing to the glaring hole Thompson cut.

Thompson turned back and said, "You know what? I've got a bright idea. Since you're already a jackass, Vadim, how's about you plow us a path, and we watch?"

Vadim was the only one who didn't laugh.

"Okay, no more funny business. Machetes out, and whatever you do, don't step on a water moccasin," Thompson said.

They hacked with machetes for miles, the hot Everglade sun endlessly beating down. Their faces showed no hint of misery, yet inside, each one screamed. A place where it rains a dozen times per day sounded like paradise compared to this slice of Floridian hell.

On and on they marched, the day slowly melting by. Blinding green in every direction yielded to liquid in the form of a swamp. Bar-Yochai took a step into the water.

Thompson said, "Easy, Bar. We're not that bold. We'll walk around it."

A splash from the water drew everyone's attention. They watched a humungous alligator tail slip beneath algae-covered waves.

"Ready and willing to swim, T. Say the word. I've always wanted to hunt a dinosaur," said Bar-Yochai. He unholstered his Beretta and aimed at the water.

"You'll just have to settle for Nazis instead," Thompson said. "We'll traverse the perimeter."

They cut around the swamp and resumed trekking through somewhat dry land, stopping only to hydrate every few kilometers. Just like in the field, nobody spoke as they walked. Their machetes did all the talking instead.

By day's end, everyone sweat harder than when the Soviets raided the safe house. Thompson never said it, but even if Uzziel hadn't perished, there was no way his aged body could have endured this boggy inferno. They would have been a fractured team regardless. Still, at least then he'd be alive.

"I think that's enough for today," Thompson announced when the sun began to sink. "Report, all."

Everyone exchanged exasperated faces, but nobody complained. "All good training," Bar-Yochai proclaimed.

"Mostly good training," Vadim remarked under his breath. His humanity couldn't be masked.

"What was that, Vadim?" Thompson asked.

"I said I'm having a grand old time with this ed-ju-ma-kay-ting," he smartly replied.

"At least your spirits have healed," Thompson said. He turned to the rest of his crew and added, "I'm pleased with how this went. It sure didn't start that way. From the time we dropped until about two hours ago, I was going to schedule a second training exercise just like this."

Vadim made a face of pure agony. Thompson continued, "But, minus Vadim's parachute episode, I don't think we'll be needing it. Training suspended until sunrise. Let's build a fire and kick back."

They converged between a towering collection of Redwood trees to observe the starry night sky. Nadir and Vadim dug a small pit, while Thompson and Herschel gathered sticks and leaves. The damp soil and humid air rendered fire kindling a challenge. And although the heat subsided, ravenous mosquitos substituted misery well into the night. Even with military-grade repellent, everyone remained harassed.

"Fucker," Vadim said as he swatted his arm. "Could be worse. I had this guy in my old Pacific unit from Minnesota. Claimed the bugs were so big they carried off his neighbor's dog. Neighbors found it drained like a vampire got to it. 'Unofficial state bird,' he'd say."

"Bugs or not, I'd take that frigid cold any day of the week," said Bar-Yochai. "Freezing to death is nothing. All you do is go to sleep as everything turns numb. Piece of cake if you ask me," he joked. "Heat? Well, there's a reason Christians say hell is hot and full of fire. Nothing worse than burning."

The chatter felt welcoming after being silent all day. Herschel lit a cigarette and said, "Speak for yourself, Bar. After three winters in Europe, I'll gladly face any heat. There's nothing like taking a bullet while you're shivering your ass off or worse, stepping over a frozen corpse. Nine times out of ten, you can tell what the poor bastard was thinking right as they died."

"Please," said Vadim. "Have either of you smelled a body after it's cooked in the hot sun for two days? I don't believe that fire and brimstone crap because I've seen worse. Jungle wars are harsher than any biblical hell." Vadim was the only one amongst them who fought in the Pacific. He witnessed all forms of atrocity and secretly considered the Japanese worse than the S.S. He'd never admit it to anyone.

Bar-Yochai promised dinner and disappeared through the trees. Twenty minutes later, a single gunshot sounded from afar. He returned shortly after with a deer slung over his shoulder. He tossed it before them like a spoil of war. "Fresh venison. My specialty," he boasted.

He dragged the carcass off into the shadows and set to work cleaning it. The sound of his knife slitting flesh and tendons cut through the hum of night-time creatures.

"Be sure to bury whatever's left. The last thing we need is a panther sniffing through here," Thompson called.

"Panther?" Vadim worriedly asked.

"Or a giant reptile or anything else could be lurking. I don't care to find out," Thompson cautioned. He piled the brush in the freshly-dug fire pit and used his lighter to birth flames. Soon a bonfire roared.

Belching smoke dissuaded most of the buzzing insects and provided a much-needed reprieve.

A blood-spattered Bar-Yochai sat down near the fire with patches of meat skewered through sticks. He laid the sticks over the fire and introduced a loud hiss as flames licked the meat. Everyone stared at the dancing embers in the soft humid breeze.

"To be correct, German Roe Deer is my specialty, but whatever the hell this is, it's got fur and four legs. I'm sure it'll do swell," Bar-Yochai said.

"You never mentioned you were a cook," Vadim said. "Hmm, I can just picture it now: Bullets-a-flyin' and you're skipping around in a skimpy little camouflage apron, serving the boys battlefield snacks," he chimed.

Bar-Yochai turned redder than he had all day. "It wasn't quite that vivid, I'm afraid," he said through clenched teeth. "I saw an animal. I shot it. I made something of it for the unit whenever I could. That's all."

"How many did you kill anyway?" Vadim asked.

"What, Germans?"

"No, your own men, from poisoning them with your cooking!"

Bar-Yochai folded his arms and confidently fired back, "I'll have you know if they gave out medals for culinary triumphs, I'd be General Fink by now."

"If you can take a bullet, you can take a joke, Bar. Relax- and that's coming from the guy who got thrown out of a plane by a belligerent Canuck."

Bar-Yochai resigned his fuming temper. They wolfed down the meat and sat quietly for a while after, listening to the crackling fire and Everglade chorus.

"I miss him horribly," Nadir said. Nobody spoke; they just mused and listened. "It wasn't supposed to happen the way it did. Not for a guy like Uzziel."

"Life isn't like chess, Nadir. You can't calculate for everything," Thompson said.

Herschel took a long sip from his flask. He breathed the booze out with a cough and muttered, "You've never been on a real battlefield, Nadir. Soldiers check-in and they check-out. It's painful. It's unjust. It's something that makes you want to scream up at the sky as if it could make a difference. All we can do is keep going and cross more names off our list. If nothing else, we don't do it for justice anymore. We do it for Uzziel. Let our bullets become his legacy."

Herschel passed the flask to Bar-Yochai. He sipped lightly and gave it to Nadir. She hadn't drunk a sip of alcohol in years. She took a wincing sip and then tossed it to Thompson. He smiled, raised the flask, and polished off the last of it.

Bar-Yochai laid back on the moist black soil. He felt so tired he could take a literal dirt nap. As Nesher Unit's oldest member, he wanted desperately to hide his age. He shut his eyes for a second, or maybe it was ten minutes. He found the group roaring with laughter at an animated Vadim in the midst of a story:

"-And as I'm trying to pry the brass out of his ass cheek, Private Jennings is so hopped up on morphine all he can do is scream 'How the fuck am I supposed to shit now?!' Meanwhile it's the infirmary from hell. I've got sixteen other men puking their guts out from the bad oatmeal, and all of them are looking at this guy like they want him to die of blood loss. Well, I get the bullet out and have the nurses isolate him so nobody can beat him up, but someone slipped laxatives into his food. This guy turns his bed into a fucking brown bathtub. It's a mess. And it doesn't just happen once. These kids managed to spike his food half a dozen more times. I was so worried he was going to get an infection and die- he was shitting himself that much! Why the hell they'd put a soldier with that low of an IQ in charge of a kitchen, I can only imagine."

Bar-Yochai drifted off again. He awoke to Thompson kicking his boot, teasing him about the precise thing he wanted to hide. "Old man, peel them bones off the ground. We're hitting the hay."

All their gear was identical to the real mission's. It included small arms, ration bars, and even prototype equipment from various branches of the military. This time they had reusable water purifiers that could boil river water as well as closeable waterproof nylon hammocks that shielded whoever slept inside.

They suspended their sleeping hammocks from the redwoods with an array of spikes and cables. Vadim found it hard to complain once comfortably on his back, safe from the molestation of blood-sucking insects. Bar-Yochai fell asleep as soon as he closed his eyes. Herschel, Vadim, and Thompson followed soon after. But Nadir laid awake for most of the night. In the darkness of her sleeping bag, all she had were memories of tragedy playing before her eyes.

She awoke in a familiar cold sweat to the sound of drizzle. The dim blue of daylight crept through the nylon fibers to color her face. It would be a muggy day's hike, but at least there wouldn't be any sun.

Nadir's movement stirred Thompson awake. He unzipped his bag and crawled down. "Up and at 'em!" he cried, clapping his hands. "It's daybreak, kids, and we've got another ten clicks until we reach the extraction point. From here on out, we're back in training mode."

Rolling clouds doused them with an increasing drizzle as they disassembled their sleeping provisions and packed everything up. Herschel left his gear resting at the base of a Redwood and trotted away.

"Where are you going?" Thompson whispered.

"To do something I haven't in a long time," Herschel said over his shoulder.

"What's that?"

"Shit in a bush."

Thompson turned to Nadir and said, "I won't patronize you, but I suggest you get acclimated to what he's describing."

"Soon as that deer gets through me, I'm sure I'll discover a new past-time," Nadir said.

They embarked north, hacking their way for miles in a repetition of the previous day's labor. The absent sun made a world of difference, for shielding clouds provided shady relief as they droned through wetlands.

By midday, the sound of squishing water beneath her boots drove Nadir mad. Then a thumping sound slashed through her frustration and diverted her attention upward. All her frustration evaporated instantly.

"There's our lift," Thompson said gingerly.

Alligators infested the swamp beach ahead. All but one vacated into the water as the Sikorsky CH-37 Mojave helicopter came thundering in. A single gunshot and ensuing eruption of sand right next to the defiant gator's head sent it retreating with its kin. The helicopter kicked up a whirlwind as it touched down on the sand.

Bar-Yochai lowered his Beretta.

"You missed," Vadim said.

"I'll save the killing for the jungle. And don't forget," he added as they climbed into the helicopter, "Drinks are on you."

CHAPTER 13
APRIL 1945 - THE NORTH SEA

ONE COULD HEAR a pin drop inside of the pressurized cabin it was so deathly quiet. All hands nervously held their breath as two American Mark-14 torpedoes hummed by in rapid succession. The bubbles generated from their thrusters sizzled outside of U-1055's hull.

Those torpedoes are going to collide with each other, Von Schwangau realized. He covered his head and cried "Down!" to his men.

A shockwave sent the submarine into a helpless tumble which briefly cut the lights. He was about to order his first seaman to adjust eighteen degrees and return fire until he thought *they might think they got us.* He put his finger to his lips and whispered, "Shh." It would be the single wisest move of his long and decorated naval career.

U-1055 was one of fifty German U-boats unaccounted for at the end of the war. Though it was never confirmed, most presumed it sunk that forlorn afternoon in April. They were sorely mistaken.

SIX MONTHS AGO – BRAZIL

Von Schwangau held a torch as he stared up at U-1055's steel hull. The hulking leviathan was housed inside of a wooden hangar on the lake, suspended in the air by a network of heavy chains. "How I've missed you," he muttered, stroking his free hand against the hull. She hadn't so much as touched the water for years.

"It really was a privilege," Yuri nervously said in broken German. Having completed the contract, he and his crew were apprehensive about what might come next. Yuri wanted to trust the man in the iron mask, but everything about this undertaking had been utterly bizarre. "Such a well-engineered machine," he added in appeasement.

A Russian butchering his sacred tongue was almost too much for Von Schwangau to stomach. That a Soviet would be the one to launch their rebirth demonstrated just how desperate the Reich's fallen heirs had become. Contract repair crews couldn't be found with ease, and when their contact in Budapest reached out to say he'd located some, Von Schwangau and the high council were all-too-eager to acquire their services. As any Nazi could attest, a body for labor was just that. He smiled an evil grin, but Yuri would never see. The only detail he ever saw of the man's face were his pale blue eyes glowing behind the mask.

He was the least of the contract's oddities. The job came through Yuri's longtime contact, Jinter Boozis. Like the rest of Jinter's contracts, it looked to be a big score. They were told a German submarine had been illicitly acquired somewhere in South America and needed significant repairs. The machine's actual use was anyone's guess. His ten-man crew could get in and out within just one month. After that, they'd enjoy some long-needed vacation time.

Yuri and company traveled from Europe to Mexico City and stayed two nights in a five-star hotel. On the third day, a call came from the lobby. The front desk attendant informed Yuri his bill was paid, and a collection of cars were waiting for his party. They took a small motorcade to a runway in the desert, where they boarded a dual-engine propeller plane.

Inside, two white men who spoke German were waiting. They poured drinks, offered cigarettes, and laughed gaily with the Russians. But somewhere over South America, the Germans turned hostile. Yuri and his crew were given blindfolds and told it was for their own safety. Yuri didn't care to think what the men would do if they refused, so he nodded for everyone to obey.

Blindfolds couldn't mask the fact they were landing on a dirt runway. *Where are we?* Yuri wondered. Stepping off the plane, he could feel the sticky wet sun above. Cawing birds and buzzing insects were all he could hear. No doubt they were somewhere secluded. *What had Jinter gotten them in to?*

Yuri and his crew were taken half a mile from the runway and told to remove their blindfolds. They found Von Schwangau, clad in his iron mask, standing in front of a massive lakeside hangar. They would never once see him lift the mask, nor did Yuri dare ask why he wore it. A glimpse of the wilted skin surrounding the mask made him think it was to hide an injury.

"I'm told most of you speak a little German," Von Schwangau first greeted them. "Do not be afraid. This is merely a discrete project, and we are taking the utmost steps to maintain secrecy. You are being paid handsomely for your expertise and discretion. If you look to the lake, you will see we've taken the liberty of making a camp for all your needs. You will work in this hangar behind me, and you will sleep in the tents over there. You will not wander around or interact with anyone other than yourselves. Anything you need, you may ask me and me alone. At the end of the project, we will fly you to any destination you choose."

Much remained a mystery over the ensuing weeks as Yuri and his crew restored the battle-ravaged U-boat. Its pocked exterior bore many battle scars, and its underbelly was scraped nearly to the point of breach from forcing itself upriver. He knew they were escaped Nazis, that much seemed obvious. Yuri and his crew were in too deep to say no, especially in the face of riches. But the one thing he couldn't ignore was the U-boat itself. *It got them away from the Allies. What more could they need it for?* They'd have a hell of a time launching it back into the ocean. Then again, if they'd gotten it in without sinking, surely, they could get it back out, too.

Several weeks passed without incident. Nobody bothered Yuri or his crew, and everything they wanted, they received. Vodka. Fresh meat. Even a fiddle. They were left alone to work. The man in the mask loomed from time to time to check progress. Sometimes Yuri watched him. He would stare for hours at the U-boat like a long-lost lover.

After four weeks of intense labor, the U-boat was primed and ready. Yuri continued to flap nervous compliments in the hangar, but all Von Schwangau could hear was the imagined sound of U-1055's engines at full thrust.

"Where will you go?" Von Schwangau suddenly asked Yuri.

"The Caribbean, maybe. I hear it's very nice."

"I meant for your next job," Von Schwangau said.

"We shall see. I certainly don't need to be scouring after a job like this," Yuri tried to say. Von Schwangau understood but listening to Yuri's poor attempt at German was like watching a Jew walk down the street with a bucket of gold.

"You're sure it's fully operational?"

"My people don't make mistakes," Yuri said. He bore his brown eyes into the eye holes of Von Schwangau's mask and looked hard for a gleam of light. Despite the torch's proximity to his face, all he saw was a speck of blue intermitted with pools of black.

Von Schwangau picked up on Yuri's searching stare and calmly said, "Do you really think we'd kill you? After all that you've done for us?"

"I beg your pardon?" Yuri scoffed. It was the most authentic-sounding German Von Schwangau had heard out of him yet.

"Relax. You did a good job. You respected our rules and our home. No doubt, you'll forget you were ever here. And if, by chance, we need you back to make more repairs, well, you see the value in this friendship? Men of your skillset don't grow on trees, after all."

Yuri felt a rush of relief. "Indeed not," he said. He realized his expression betrayed him and tensed his cheek muscles to deal Von Schwangau a firm gaze. "This has been good business."

"A true pleasure. All you'll have to do from here is tell the pilot where to go. The money is already on board." He reached into his pocket and handed Yuri a blindfold.

Yuri stared at it apprehensively.

"I'm sure you understand. Please," Von Schwangau said.

Yuri tied the blindfold around his eyes. Von Schwangau took him by the arm and led him out of the cavernous hangar.

Outside, the sun was just about to break over the horizon. Yuri froze when he realized they were walking toward the water.

"It's a seaplane, you idiot. I won't make you suffer that horrid runway again," Von Schwangau dully said.

Yuri shrugged off his worry and kept following Von Schwangau. He couldn't see them, but his whole blindfolded crew waited by the shore. They were oblivious to the seven Nazi youths standing around them. Each cradled a black MP-40 submachine gun in their arms.

Von Schwangau stopped Yuri at the water's edge and announced, "We thank you for your service, all of you. Go straight into the water and swim ten yards out. Climb aboard the plane, and off you go. The pilot will instruct you when it's safe to remove your blindfolds."

There was no plane, but none of the Russians could see that. Yuri took the first step into the water. His top welder, Boris, waded in behind him, steadily followed by the rest. Once they were all waist deep, Von Schwangau signaled the youths. They aimed their MP-40s and spat a hot chorus of death to greet the coming Brazilian daylight.

"Should we gather the bodies, sir?" one of the boys asked in German. Gentle wisps of smoke twirled from his red-hot MP-40 barrel. The murky lake water colored red around their floating, bullet-ravaged bodies.

"Field defense tactics. Take note, all. Their bodies feed the caimans and give them taste for human flesh. Attackers can forget any chance of water infiltration. Cadets," Von Schwangau called, "Report to your barracks for weapons cleaning and uniform swap. Physical fitness begins in thirty minutes."

"Heil Hitler!" the youths cried in Nazi salute. They ran uniformly back toward the village barracks.

Von Schwangau looked out at the water and listened to the caimans tearing apart the dead crew. With the U-boat now fully operational, just one piece of the puzzle remained until the Iron Eagle could unleash global terror again.

CHAPTER 14

VADIM'S EYES remained shut throughout the entire patch of turbulence. He tried to imagine the cabin's vibration as the beautiful woman he bedded right after the Everglades.

Thompson issued one day of leave, which Vadim spent chasing tail. Her crimson dress looked like a blooming rose amidst the bar's dying bush of low lives, tramps, and fiends. He confidently approached to strike up a conversation but touching her soft freckled skin left him tongue-tied. "My goodness," he managed to squeak, "What do you charge for a handshake?"

They laughed, danced, and by sunrise, they'd made love more times than Vadim could count. The beauty's warm red nipples tickling his cheeks felt like heaven on earth.

Then he remembered he was actually up in the heavens, and those same cheeks were almost swelling with vomit as the plane dropped a few hundred feet in altitude.

"One minute! Positions!" Thompson cried. A roar took the cabin as the cargo doors peeled open to reveal puffy clouds bathed in white moonlight.

"Hang on a minute!" a voice shouted. One of the co-pilots peered back in the cargo hold. "Look, we were told not to ask what's going on here, but the pilot and I agree this isn't safe. We're picking up a big storm that wasn't formed when we took off."

Thompson looked apprehensively at his crew. "We can still abort but diverting a supply plane over the coordinates was no easy feat. This might be our one and only shot."

"Let's just go for it," Herschel said. Bar-Yochai nodded agreeably.

"Goddammit," Vadim muttered. The open cargo doors were loud enough to mask his comment. He wouldn't back down; he didn't have to enjoy it either.

"Sorry, but we've got a job to do, Thompson told the co-pilot.

"Your funerals," the co-pilot said.

"Maybe we should abort. We never trained for a storm," Nadir yelled.

"A little water never hurt anyone," Herschel yelled back.

"You forget the story of Noah's Ark!" Vadim said.

"And you forget Noah lived! Nobody's even shooting at us. Toughen up!"

A green light shined over the cargo doors. Thompson said, "Stay if you want. I won't hold it against anyone. Otherwise, that's our signal, people!"

"Me first," Herschel said, stopping Thompson. He dove out with his arms extended.

Thompson watched him go and cried, "For Uzzie!" He crossed his arms and dropped straight back out of the plane. Bar Yochai followed a second later. Nadir and Vadim were left worriedly staring at each other.

<hr />

At first, Thompson couldn't tell direction. Only when he stole a glance of the half-crescent moon did he affirm spatial orientation. The air grew thicker with each passing second.

He spotted Herschel plunge through the clouds a few hundred

yards below. Thompson shifted his body to match Herschel's trajectory and shot through the clouds behind him.

Moisture consumed him as blinding light flashed from every direction. Once he realized it was lightning, every hair on his body stood straight up.

He fell through darkness interluded with flares of electricity and loud snapping thunderclaps. It was the power of Adonai, and Thompson was at his mercy. One ill-fated eclectic-fingered flick and he was dead.

Silence greeted him at the bottom cloud layer. It was the eeriest form of tranquility imaginable. It felt as if he were inside of a peaceful bubble, and all around him, there was war.

Serenity shattered as he broke free of the clouds. Elements barraged him with bashful wind and blinding rain. Only then did he consider the drop to be an egregious error. This was no ordinary storm, and they still had a mile of exposure until touchdown. Thompson could only wonder with helpless horror how the rest were faring.

A bolt of lightning streaked from the heavens down to the forest, incinerating a tree and narrowly missing Thompson in its path. He'd have to use the burning tree like a beacon to judge when to pull his ripcord.

"Here we go," Thompson said to himself. He yanked the ripcord and braced as the chute sprawled out.

A wind gust violently jerked him through the air. Up and down he flew. He must have caught a hole in the draft because suddenly he found himself descending in a controlled manner over the Amazon river.

"Not good," Thompson said again. He was going to land right in the middle of the river. Entanglement in the water meant certain death, not to mention whatever wildlife might be lurking in its depths.

He narrowly steered clear of the water and landed in a roll along the sludgy riverbank. The rain battered down and washed the mud clean as he set to work wrapping up his parachute. Lightning flashes combined with pounding rain made for a cascade of sensation. His displacement was now the least of his worries. He felt confident he could navigate to the rendezvous point. How the rest of the team made it could be another question entirely.

CHAPTER 15

I REALLY COULD GET USED to this rush, Nadir thought. It felt as if she were an invincible hawk tumbling effortlessly through the sky. The drop over the Everglades seemed like a dream. But this time she realized it might become a nightmare. Gleaming moonlight rendered the storm's severity impossible to detect. Only up close could she discern the clouds were alive with lightning.

She punched through the top ceiling and lost all visibility an inch beyond her nose. Her only sensations were lightning flashes, the howling wind ripping against her ears, and loud thunderclaps booming from all directions.

She felt a hand squeeze her wrist. Her heart fluttered as Bar-Yochai pulled himself right up to her face. Vadim joined a moment later to form a triangle.

"We're okay!" Bar-Yochai shouted.

They encountered a layer of stillness. Above, lightning refused to cease, but the thunder sounded as if it were a distant affair far, far away.

"Do not let go!" Bar-Yochai shouted. The bottom layer obliterated all sense of tranquility. Gusting wind and beating rain assaulted their triangle. Meanwhile sporadic lightning illuminated the widening jungle below.

"Just stay calm!" Bar-Yochai screamed. "Ten more seconds!" A sudden updraft annihilated Nadir's grip. It felt as if her guts were being ripped out through her navel. She disappeared in a heartbeat through soaking sheets of rain.

"Nadir!" they vainly shouted. Bar-Yochai grabbed Vadim's ripcord, yelled, "No choice!" and pulled it.

Bar-Yochai cast off to chase after Nadir. A burning tree in the forest indicated he only had a few seconds to activate his parachute. He zipped through the air, back and forth, but Nadir was gone. He had to yield.

"You're in God's hands now," he said in Hebrew. He pulled his ripcord with seconds to spare.

CHAPTER 16

THOMPSON'S FRUSTRATION simmered to a boiling point. This place felt markedly worse than the Everglades, for at least there, the weather made up its mind. Here, the rain came sporadically, sometimes numerous times per hour. He went from dirty to cleansed to filthy again, and now the scorching sun stabbed through the thick trees to fry whatever remained of his sanity. He had no idea how far off course his comrades landed, or if they survived at all.

"This was such a mistake," he admitted to no one. He had been walking with a machete in one hand and his 1911 in the other. The sight of a giant anaconda sunning along the riverbank unnerved him enough to keep his sidearm poised.

He couldn't help the harsh climate making sloth of his pace. He checked his Lensatic compass every few hundred paces. At his current speed, he might reach the rendezvous point- a fork in the river- within the next few hours. He certainly wasn't concerned with stealth anymore. It only took one kilometer of hiking for him to harbor doubt that anyone could survive this hostile ecosystem.

He stopped to drink from his reusable canteen. He'd have to thank General Fink for finding legitimately useful equipment to test. If he lost or broke it, his odds of survival would dwindle.

He finished the first canteen and scooped it full of river water. He'd consume the other one throughout his hike and boil them both at dusk.

Hours passed. As the sun started to arch behind the trees, he took out a silk-printed map. Most of this region had only been charted from the air. It was still better than wandering blind. He knelt in the dirt and compared the crude map against his compass. If correct, the fork was just around the next bend. That meant if he hacked his way through what appeared only to be a few acres of the jungle-

He abandoned the idea ten exhausting minutes later. The trees were far too dense to make so much as a dent. He returned to the river bank and continued wandering along its shoreline with a sore arm, hoping to hell he didn't run into another giant snake.

His mind wandered through combat flashbacks: Scattered severed limbs in the streets of Kassel; witnessing a young private lose the top-half of his head after peering around a wall in battle; Thompson turning over the bodies of machine-gunned Germans, only to discover most were teenagers...

He wondered how old he'd have to grow until the flashbacks stopped.

When he took off his uniform, or when he entered his grave?

Suddenly the buzzing insects grew noticeably lurid. He stopped when he realized it wasn't mosquitos he heard: it sounded more like flies.

He took a few more steps and stopped. The sweet, revolting stench of death ransacked his nostrils to elicit a gag reflex. He plugged his nose and hacked a hole in the jungle toward the sound. The noise and smell became worse with each machete swing.

Thompson scoffed when he saw it, thinking back to Vadim's jungle corpse remarks in the Everglades. Dew and maggots soaked a mess of rotting red flesh and wilted bone. The maggots devoured with such ravenous voracity that the corpse shook. On cold battlefields, Thompson remembered death's scent to be mild. Correct to Vadim's caution, in this sticky wet heat, death's nauseating intensity exacerbated tenfold.

Through the blanket of flies and maggots, Thompson could see the body wore a logo work jacket. He didn't dare venture close to inspect details. He was on the verge of puking, and his body couldn't afford such a taxing expense.

As Thompson retreated a few steps back, he felt pressure underneath his boot heel. He removed his boot to find a shiny brass casing nestled in the soil. He kneeled and scooped it up out of the moist dirt.

Terror flared as his eyes stole down the casing's exterior. The bottom of the casting bore a head-stamp code, 2*dnh*- indicating the factory number; and *1944*- indicating the year it was made. He knew this spent shell all too well. He'd stepped over countless other examples as he stormed the streets of Germany a decade ago.

CHAPTER 17

THE OTHER CHILDREN BELIEVED. They didn't even question it. But
Nadir was not the same as them. She was a realist, a thinker, a cynic
to the point that her elders considered her the walking definition of
an "old soul." No matter how hard she tried, she just couldn't get
herself to believe in God.

"What is it you find so outlandish about a creator?" her Rabbi
once asked. The year was 1938 as the Rabbi interviewed all the
Hebrew school children in preparation for their bar and bat mitzvahs.

"Look around," Nadir wallowed in their private meeting. "What
kind of God allows his people to suffer like this?"

"It's all part of his plan," the Rabbi explained. "What you see in
politics- The atrocities you witness in the streets- Nothing is for
naught in the way of Adonai. To the untrained eye, this may look like
the beginning of the end. Rest assured, child- it is anything but. God's
grace is all around us. You just have to look closely."

"I'll believe it when I see it," she coldly replied. Many months
later, she traded glances with the Rabbi as he was stuffed aboard a
cattle car bound for the death camps. She wondered about God
then. Based upon the Rabbis' expression, so did he. She never
thought much of her escape from that horrid ghetto as divine inter-

vention. Only years later when Rafa laid out the facts did she reconsider.

But now, after falling through the heavens without so much as a scratch, Nadir felt genuinely pious. If it weren't for a sudden updraft, her parachute wouldn't have saved her.

She hung suspended from the branch of a massive Wimba tree. It looked far too high for her to jump down. She remained battered by rain until daybreak. Once she had a little light, she started pulling herself up the branch. As soon as she heard a cracking sound, she said, "Oh no."

The branch snapped. She plummeted fifty feet, stopping just before she hit the ground. Her parachute snagged on another branch, sparing her from death but painfully straining her body from the shock. She exhaled with relief and pulled out a knife to slit herself free.

She gathered up as much of the ragged parachute as she could. She fell trying to jump and snatch the last few bits. She picked her head off the ground to see a train of ants dragging a giant dead spider into their mound. She peeled herself off the forest floor in fright.

She cocked and locked the Browning's safety with an upward stroke of her thumb and stuck it in her belt line. Then she took out her Lensatic compass and nearly screamed. The impact left it shattered. All she had was a crude map printed on silk fabric.

She planted her machete blade-down in the soil and poured over the map. "We dropped over here," she began while tracing a finger. "Hit the storm... And now I'm... somewhere over here. Maybe."

On the ground, the trees were thick enough to blot out the sun. Navigating without a compass would be a tricky business. She knew she couldn't stay put. She also knew an incorrect guess could prove to be just as fatal. During the war, every person she encountered lusted to take her life. Out here, the same was true, only with every plant and animal added into the mix. If she could find the Amazon river, she could find the team.

The foliage varied from thick in some patches and thin in others.

She moved between the narrowest trees conserve energy. It didn't stop her stomach from growling after just a few hours hiking. She hadn't had anything to eat since they took off from Texas. She fished a ration bar out her backpack, scarfed it down, and tucked the wrapper away.

The day dolled by slowly. Sweat fowled her whole body as the sun started to sink in the late afternoon. The only water she'd located thus far had come from above. She knew she'd soon have to make camp for the night. She'd need to find a large tree for the highest possible sleeping quarters. The thought of slumbering on a midnight jungle floor sent chills down her spine.

She hoped to find another Wimba tree laden with vines for an easy climb. But after an hour of searching, all the trees were starting to blur, and she remained empty-handed.

Suddenly she found herself in a massive artificial clearing. She rubbed her eyes in disbelief. All the trees had been cut down and neatly stacked in piles. She walked to the middle of the empty site where she found a massive crater that looked as if dynamite had been set off.

"What is this?" she wondered aloud. There were abandoned tools all over the ground. She picked up a hand saw and read the words "*PATLAY MINING CO*" printed on its side. There wasn't much grime on it, meaning it hadn't been there for long. There were also numerous footprints about the scene, with no bodies to match them. *Where was everyone?*

A lump appeared in her throat the instant her brain processed the sound of buzzing flies. She'd seen enough carnage in her life to know exactly what it meant.

She thumbed the Browning's safety off and defensively held it in front of her. She peered over a bush and shut her eyes before they could drink in the gory details. There were several dead bodies. The jungle had gotten to them, and mutilated pieces were all that remained.

Nadir darted behind a log as she heard the sound of breaking branches.

"They'll be back," a voice warned in German.

"And when they come, they will be dealt with. And whoever comes after will suffer the same fate. Eventually, they'll give up," a second voice replied.

"The company might still investigate."

"I am wholly unconcerned with whatever repercussions a mining company has in store. Given how ill-equipped their workers were, I bet they'd sooner cut their losses than send another group."

"You forget, those Yankees are nothing but stubborn pigs. I bet they send three more groups in before they give up."

The men were venturing close. Nadir shoved a hand over her mouth to mute her breathing.

"Why are we back here again?"

"I need to know for certain."

"You shot him three times. Even if he escaped, he couldn't have survived. He's probably been eaten by a thousand different things. There's nothing left to find."

"I want to be damn sure."

The voices trailed off.

Nadir poked her head up to steal a glance over the log.

Two tall white men sporting camouflaged hunting cloaks were walking with pistols in their hands. Nadir ducked back down as one of the men turned back in her direction.

Her heart started pounding. She ducked before he could turn his face, but Nadir was sure it was him. It took everything not to scream out after laying eyes on Hermann Michel, in the flesh.

There was no way she could apprehend them both, but if she could sneak around and ambush them...

Their footsteps were no longer audible. Nadir closed her eyes to heighten her hearing. The jungle chorus proved too loud.

She opened her eyes and decided to chance another glance over the log.

"Good evening, young lady," a Germanic voice said from behind. Nadir's eyes went wide when she heard the cock of a pistol.

"Lower your weapon and turn around, please," the other voice said.

Nadir outstretched her arm with a finger wrapped around the trigger. She had seconds to make up her mind. If she complied, it meant certain death. But if she missed...

She used not to believe, but once again, Nadir Horowitz was at the mercy of Adonai.

CHAPTER 18

As DAYLIGHT BEGAN TO FADE, Thompson realized how long he'd been marching. He was still determined to reach the rendezvous point, even if darkness came first.

At twilight's zenith, their shapes came into form at the fork in the river. Thompson felt his nerves ease until he counted three figures, and not four. It only took a few more steps to deduce the slenderest was missing. "Where is she?" he beckoned once he came within earshot of Bar-Yochai, Herschel, and Vadim.

"We don't know," Herschel replied grimly.

"A draft whisked her away. Bar tried to go after her, but it was too dangerous. God only knows where she landed," Vadim said.

"Vadim and I found Herschel here a few hours ago," Bar-Yochai said. "So far, we haven't found anything except trees and rain."

"She got spun like a top up there. Even if she's unhurt, she's probably very lost. We should go searching now that we're all together," Vadim said.

Thompson jittered. "I'm afraid it's more complicated than that."

"What do you mean?" Bar-Yochai asked.

"I have to show you something," Thompson said. He took out the

Walther shell casing and tossed it to Bar-Yochai. "There's a body rotting face down on the forest floor a few clicks back. Probably three or four days old. I found that in the dirt nearby."

"Holy hell," Vadim said, taking the shell casing from Bar-Yochai. His eyes dazzled as he turned it every which way. He handed it to Herschel and said, "What are the odds of finding German brass all the way out here?"

A distant gunshot echoed through the trees. Everyone froze and looked up.

"That sounded a thousand meters off, at least," Herschel whispered.

"What if it's Nadir?" Vadim whispered back.

"It's almost dark. We have to stay put," Thompson said.

"Are you nuts?" Vadim objected. "We can't ignore that with Nadir still missing."

"What if it's a trap? There are a million reasons not to go running off."

"And one reason to," Vadim said.

"For all we know, it wasn't even Nadir. She might still show up at this spot, and then what? We'll make camp for the night, and in the morning, we'll check it out. That's an order."

"Yes sir," all three said; Vadim least enthusiastically.

They unpacked gear and got to work hanging up sleeping hammocks. Everyone quietly got in and nestled for a harrowing night's sleep.

They'd all slept on numerous battlefields and were well-versed in the art of distress, but this felt unworldly. The deafening animal screams and ever-changing weather patterns made sleep nearly impossible. Near daybreak, a downpour so fierce rolled through, Vadim feared they'd all wash away. He only slept for forty minutes the entire night.

"Vadim," Thompson said, shattering his brief dream state.

"Mmm?" he grumbled. He'd temporarily forgotten all that transpired.

"Wake up. It's nearly light."

They took precaution not to leave so much as a broken twig in their wake. They ate a few ration bars, hydrated, dusted themselves with insect repellant, and then waited patiently. Half of the day elapsed. Nadir failed to arrive.

"I say we go looking," Vadim suggested. "We've got less than seventy hours until extraction. We're wasting time, Thompson. Nadir would have made it by now if she was okay."

"Forget it. I'm not breaking protocol," Thompson said.

Vadim's sleeplessness transmuted to anger. "What is wrong with you? Every second we sit here, she might be getting more lost! If we run out of time before we find her, she's gone forever."

"That was a single shot we heard. If anyone were chasing her, there would have been more," Thompson said.

"My guess is someone was hunting," Bar-Yochai said. "If anyone is living out here, they live off the land. It's the only way to stay hidden. That said, I agree with Vadim, Thompson. I think having a look around might be the best course."

"Fine," Thompson said resentfully. "Herschel, give us your best guess as to where that shot came from."

"The Hammer" was initially trained as an army ranger. Land navigation had been the bread and butter of his schooling. If anyone knew how to calculate gunfire at a distance, it would be him. He discerned options and pointed the direction of his best guess, indicating east.

"Alright, you heard the man," Thompson said. "Let's move, team."

The temperature sweltered to a Fahrenheit that made the previous day seem mild by comparison. It didn't take long for everyone to get caked in mud and sweat. Concealing every step proved most irritating, but they took no chances now. Even chatter reduced to whispers, and only at Thompson's discretion.

It took three hours of silent hiking for Vadim to snap. "These birds are driving me fucking wild!" he fumed.

"Shh!" Thompson scowled from the front of the line.

"Nobody could ever hear us over all of this extra noise, Thompson," Vadim said. "I can't even hear myself think, for Christ's sake."

"That's the heat, you idiot," Bar-Yochai mumbled.

"Hey, aren't you supposed to be the doctor here?" Herschel said to Vadim. He holstered any further jibes upon looking back at him.

Vadim resembled the very picture of a man stuck in hell; sweat dribbled off his beat-red face down soggy wet hair, and skin smeared with mud, red splotches showing through to reveal his overheated complexion.

"You should drink some water," Herschel suggested.

"Let's all do that," Thompson said.

As they gathered under the base of a Brazilian nut tree, a thunderclap sang from the skies. "Guess we'll be getting another shower then, too. Can't say I'm sore about it," Thompson said.

Vadim closed his eyes as the rain drenched them. "Fuck, that feels good," he said, washing the mud off his skin and hair.

"I'd say we've covered a thousand meters," Bar-Yochai remarked. "And I'm sorry to say, but I don't believe this was where the shot originated."

"How can you tell? Everything looks the damn same out here," Vadim said.

Thompson put his hands to his hips. "This wasn't part of the plan, and now we're wasting more precious time by wandering around. We'll try one more direction, and then we'll head back to the rendezvous point and wait. If she doesn't show by tomorrow, we'll go from there. Herschel, give us your next guess."

Herschel looked up at the trees and said, "It's tough to determine exactly. Hills can mess with how sound travels, not to mention all the trees." He pointed to a large gap in the foliage where two distant hills poked through to eclipse the cloudy skies. "Those hills over there? I'd say that's worth a try."

Thompson stopped. "*Try?*" he asked.

"My chips on are all on black here, T."

Thompson rubbed his eyes in frustration. "Right. Because you do so well with that, just like in Malta," he said, a stern frown dampening his rare sarcasm.

A year prior, Nesher Unit tracked a Nazi fugitive to a casino in Malta. Thompson gave each member $200 of his own money to gamble with and blend in. The first thing Herschel did was bet it all on black, and well...

Herschel scoffed. "Hey, you asked for my second guess, there it is. Otherwise, the rendezvous is still a dozen beads back," he said, pointing.

They made haste in the direction of the hills. A steep incline marred by thick trees obstructed the way and decimated their fast pace. It took over an hour, and once they made it to the summit, even with machetes, there was no way to cut through. Then they encountered a blind drop over a cliff. It looked as if something had taken a magic eraser to the earth.

"Should we turn back?" Vadim asked.

"Nonsense," Thompson said. "Follow my lead." He scaled the cliff ledge by gripping the trees and carefully placing his feet. "Just don't look down," he said.

One by one, the rest followed around the cliff. Nobody dared to discern its depth. Fatality didn't require a specific height assessment.

Halfway around, Vadim worriedly said, "Hey, guys?"

Bar-Yochai was the only one who heard. He turned to see a yellow pit viper staring Vadim in the face.

"Vadim, do not move," Bar-Yochai warned. He used his free hand to pull a stainless-steel throwing knife out of his breast pouch.

"No. Bar, don't you dare!" Vadim pleaded. He slammed his eyes shut as the blade stuck in the tree right by his head. He looked over to see the viper impaled on the knife.

"All on black!" Bar-Yochai hooted. "I want that knife back, too."

They kept climbing for what felt like an hour. Right as it seemed they'd reached the end, another bend would reveal even more distance to cover. Eventually, a large cavity in the trees provided a reprieve. They climbed in the hundred-square-foot space and rested their aching hands. The view offered a bird's eye glimpse of the entire rainforest valley.

"Well, I'd say this isn't right," Vadim said. "And now we've managed to get ourselves stuck."

"At least this provides a good vantage point," Bar-Yochai remarked. "Look how high we are now. We can assess the whole valley."

Herschel split over the ledge. His loogie spun and came apart in the wind, its fragments disappearing into the green abyss.

Thompson pulled out a camouflage-colored spy scope and began surveying the valley. He took out the silk map and added, "I don't even see where we are on the map anymore."

Bar-Yochai took it upon himself to keep scaling the cliff. "I'll be right back," he said. He returned ten minutes later bearing a grim face. "This thing goes on as far as I can see."

Herschel joined Thompson at the ledge. "Look at all this ground left to cover," he said. "If we wanted to do a thorough search out here, we'd need months, not days." Herschel sat down in the cavity and took out his water canteen.

Thompson silently surveyed a while longer. It wasn't just the heat. Staring at this massive green expanse, the mission seemed utterly futile. *How could they ever hope to accomplish anything with so much ground to cover and so little time?*

"If we want to make it back to the river fork by nightfall, we should get moving," Bar-Yochai suggested.

Just as Thompson lowered his spy scope, a shiny gleam caught his eye in the valley. "Hang on," he said. He raised the spy scope again and looked a moment longer. "Bar, come here," he urged.

Bar-Yochai joined Thompson at the cliff with his binoculars.

"Eleven O'clock," Thompson said, pointing down to the valley. "That big hole in the trees. Do you see what I see?"

Bar-Yochai scanned. Tangled in a mess of vines and vegetation, he could see the silver remnants of a plane wreckage.

"I'll be damned," he said.

"What is it?" Vadim asked.

"That, my friends, is a downed plane," Bar-Yochai said. "Absolutely, without question, there is something strange going on out here."

CHAPTER 19

NADIR WOEFULLY UNDERESTIMATED the prowess of the men telling her to turn around. They didn't even need to see her finger on the Browning's trigger to know what she was about to attempt.

Barbie adjusted his Walther P38 and fired a single bullet to the right side of Nadir's head. Her hearing zapped from her right ear as the bang forced her to drop her gun. She clutched her ear as tears spilled down her face. *I'll make a vengeful ghost,* she thought. She repeated it in her head, determined to make it her very last thought on earth.

"My God," Hermann said when he saw her face. They hadn't witnessed an exhibit of her kind in almost a decade. The very sight of one sent a harrowing thrust straight down their spines.

"Jew!" Barbie breathed in disbelief. He first turned to Hermann, searching for words, and then looked back at Nadir. Every hideous instinct slithering about his twisted soul screamed *kill.* His eyebrows pranced as he contemplated his next move. "Who are you?" he asked in a disturbed voice.

Nadir wore a stupefied expression. She hadn't realized it was *Klaus Barbie* walking with Hermann. Never in a million years did she expect to be face-to-face with the "Butcher of Lyon," a coveted target which Nesher Unit had been utterly clueless to track.

"Answer me!" Barbie exclaimed. "Rat or not, I know a German when I see one. Don't pretend you can't understand me!"

"We should just shoot her," Hermann said.

"Shoot her?! Look at the gear she's got on! No, I think we found this one before she found us."

Even in the face of death, training dictated intelligence. Nadir noticed they did not look the part of jungle nomads in the least bit. Not only were both men clean-shaven and fit, but their camouflage hunting cloaks and uniforms beneath were also crisp and clean too. She also noted black tilted swastikas sewn over the left breasts of their cloaks.

If they have amenities and uniforms, then that means...

"Maybe she's searching for the miners?" Hermann said.

Barbie's sinister laugh chilled Nadir to the bone. "Listen to yourself," he chuckled, "A *Jew girl* shows up all the way out here just three days later? I think not, my good Hermann. This one is military. But why they'd send her, though..."

Barbie stared piercingly. "How many others are out there, Jew?"

Nadir remained quiet. Her mind raced scenarios, and none ended well. Barbie raised his pistol and pressed the steel right up against her left eyelid.

"I will ask one more time, Jew. How many of your vermin friends are out there?"

Her right ear was still ringing, but the left one worked fine. Barbie's words revolted her to nausea. All her hatred came bubbling to life in the form her reply: "Hundreds."

Barbie and Hermann exchanged looks. Then Barbie broke out laughing. "You see? She is military! Anyone else would have told the truth."

"You don't believe her?"

"Of course not! I know a liar's eyes all too well."

"So, should we shoot her then?"

Barbie stared hard at Nadir. It had been so long since he killed one. All he had to do was pull the trigger, but her presence signified the Reich's worst fear come to life.

"Not just yet," Barbie said. "I think we need to have a lengthy conversation with her first. Sadly, this is hardly the place, and these are hardly the hospitalities."

Barbie pulled the gun away, flipped it over in his hand, and smacked Nadir over the head with the butt end. "Help me carry her," he said.

Hermann grabbed Nadir by the legs. Together they carried her off into the tropical night.

CHAPTER 20

"Assuming we can keep up this pace- and I doubt we will- I'd say we're at least a day's hike from the extraction point," Bar-Yochai said. "We don't have time. I vote no."

Command was rarely a democratic process, but in this case, Thompson felt unsure about a course of action. "Herschel?" he asked.

"Sorry, but it's safe to say I don't have an inkling about the gunshot, and we've already wasted the whole day looking. That we found something at all is just dumb luck. If we want to go check out that crash site, then the search for Nadir is off. So, I vote no."

Thompson looked to Vadim. He shook his head and said, "No way."

Thompson stared down at the airplane wreckage and said, "We'll document our findings from up here and keep moving. Vadim, you know what to do."

Vadim swung his backpack around and knelt to assemble his camera. As he aimed over the cliff to snap photos, Bar-Yochai said, "We don't have more than two or three hours of daylight, and those clouds are rolling in fast. If it starts raining while we're climbing, we could slip."

"I honestly don't think I could scale back anyway. I need rest," Thompson admitted. "We'll make camp up here and move out at first light."

A storm moved in just as the sun started to disappear over the horizon. The first thunderclap sent birds erupting from the trees to chase the vanishing daylight.

"Who'd have thought hell could be so pretty?" Vadim said.

Herschel smirked. "Insufferable heat, poisonous animals, maybe even some Nazis? Sounds like hell to me, pal."

Nightfall colored the forest turquoise, but the sordid heat refused to break. Bar-Yochai and Thompson sat at the ledge to watch the valley turn dark. "I can't help but wonder about that plane," Bar Yochai said in a hushed voice. They had to be cautious about their voices carrying through the valley.

"I bet it's been there for a couple of years," Thompson said.

"It's hard to tell from up here, but it looked fiberglass. That makes it too sleek to be a farm plane. Maybe it was private, out for a cruise over the forest. Probably dipped down to get a better view. Someone spotted it from the ground and thought they were discovered, so they brought it down."

"The question is, with what? The only thing capable is an anti-aircraft gun."

Bar-Yochai frowned. "Out here, a gun like that would rust inside of a month. It'd need good sturdy shelter to stay prime."

"So, if they do have an anti-aircraft gun..." Thompson started.

"Then it means they have a base." A grave expression besieged both of their faces. They mused in silence until it started to drizzle. At the first lighting flash, Thompson said, "I'm turning in. We've got a lot of ground to cover, so I suggest everyone do the same."

Herschel and Vadim wordlessly followed Thompson into their sleeping hammocks. Bar-Yochai remained vigilant at the ledge.

"You've got first watch, Bar?" Vadim asked.

"Yeah, I'll wake someone in a few hours for second shift," he said. A plunge in air pressure cracked the evening heat in a matter of minutes. Bar-Yochai sat unmoved as the drizzle turned to steady rainfall.

His body craved alcohol and nicotine. He slapped a mosquito and muttered, "This fucking place." He'd endured all congress of foul climates over his military career, but never like this. It was as if Adonai had pondered the single most horrid environment imaginable, and then brought it to life.

His droopy eyes grew heavy. He allowed them to briefly close as the beating rain washed the sweat from his face. He rubbed his eyes in disbelief upon opening them. Down in the forest, he spotted a tiny red glimmer moving through the trees. *Firefly* was his first thought until a second light flickered to life next to it.

Sleepiness vacated from his mind as he grabbed his binoculars. The trees were thick, but the fire from two torches was unmistakable.

"Thompson!" Bar-Yochai whispered. He dashed away from the ledge and whispered up to his sleeping comrades, "Guys! Guys, get up! Quick!"

Thompson poked his head out of his sleeping hammock and asked, "What is it?"

"We've got activity in the forest," Bar-Yochai hushed.

They collected at the ledge to watch the two torches moving through the trees.

"I'll be damned," Thompson muttered. "That's all the proof we need."

"They're right by the plane," Bar-Yochai said. "What should we do?"

"Not a damn thing but go back to sleep," Thompson said. "Make no mistake. No matter what happens next, we will be coming back here."

CHAPTER 21

THE AIR FELT DAMP, cold and stale. Nadir didn't need to open her eyes to know she was somewhere deep underground. She was sure her captors were going to shoot her, but the bump on her forehead told a much different story.

She opened her eyes to find a quiet dungeon sparsely lit by torchlight shining through the iron bars of a cell. Roots peeked through the walls in uneven patches, some sprouting through tiny cracks. Others seemed determined to reclaim the entire chamber.

Nadir peeled herself off the dirt floor. Between the cell bars, she saw a full glass of water. It had been so long since her last sip her throat felt like it was on fire. Her training decreed to withhold, but mortal instinct screamed *drink*.

She gulped down the water and then turned the empty glass in her hand. *Who left it for her?* She looked back to the entryway with curious eyes. Nobody guarded her.

She set the glass on the dirt floor and then tore off a piece of cloth from her shirt to wrap it up. She placed her foot over the fabric to break the glass, but before she could step on it, voices echoed beyond the chamber. She froze and looked up.

"Ah, good! Our specimen is awake!" cheered a male voice in boisterous German.

Nadir kept her gaze fixed on the floor. If they saw her hiding the glass beneath her foot, she lost her only shot at escape. She delicately applied pressure to mush it into the dirt.

"I trust they didn't beat you too hard, Jew," the man said.

She looked up to face the speaker. Doctor Josef Mengele, the "Angel of Death," looked as he did in wartime photos. A group of blonde-haired, blue-eyed teenagers stood about his side with notepads and pencils in their hands. All but two were boys, and each had a black swastika sewn over the left breasts of their uniforms.

"Class, today's lesson will consist of interrogation tactics. I know most of you have never seen a live one before, but please, try to contain your excitement." The Nazi cadets beamed at his words.

Dr. Mengele handed a torch to a cadet and unlocked the cell door with a skeleton key. "Now Jew, do us all a favor and relax. We have just a few questions, and these young minds are so hungry to learn."

Nadir removed her foot from the cloth and tempted grabbing the glass. She counted ten, plus the doctor. She knew she didn't stand a chance at overtaking them all. A glass dagger wouldn't make a hint of difference. She retreated to the corner; the dark cloth was dirty enough to camouflage it from her captors.

"You see, class, like any other beast, when a Jew is threatened, it will always retreat with its back to a wall," Dr. Mengele said.

They circled Nadir like hungry sharks. One misstep and someone might crunch the hidden glass.

"Fortunately, we Germans with our superior minds always overcome their primitive ways." Dr. Mengele's smile warped to a scowl with disturbing haste. "Get on the ground! This is futile!"

"I've got to try!" Nadir shouted. She'd sooner die than let a gang of Nazis have their way with her.

"Are they always this feisty, *Reichsmarschall?*" one of the two girls asked.

"*Reichsmarschall?*" thought Nadir. She recognized the old Nazi title of number two in command and briefly pondered what it could mean.

"No," Dr. Mengele answered the youth in a disappointed voice. "Take note, class. This one is far more defiant than the common specimen."

"Stay back!" Nadir warned. The youths all smiled.

"At once, converge and hold her down," Dr. Mengele instructed. "Now!"

The Nazis attacked from either side and easily seized Nadir. They held her down against the muddy floor as she screamed out in protest. One of the youths shoved his hand over her mouth to silence her. Her teeth sank right into his exposed flesh and sent him into an ear-piercing scream.

"*Reichsmarschall* Mengele! She bit me!" the boy cried, kicking Nadir in the ribs.

Dr. Mengele extracted a syringe from his white lab coat and shoved the needle into Nadir's neck. He plunged the contents into her veins and withdrew the syringe. "Let her go. Everyone out," he instructed.

The youths eased their grip and withdrew from the cell. Nadir gasped on the ground, a hand covering her neck where the needle hole leaked a tiny dab of blood.

"Siegfried, go see the infirmary about that wound," Dr. Mengele told the youth.

"But Doctor, I want to watch-"

"Now, child! A Jew bite is no laughing matter!" His face flared red, dead eyes burrowing right into Nadir's.

Siegfried retreated from the chamber cupping his bloody hand. The rest gathered to watch Nadir like she was an animal in a cage.

Nadir braced for pain. Dr. Mengele was a cruel man known for his torturous, evil concoctions; several of which served as interrogation weapons in Nesher Unit's arsenal. Surely whatever he injected her with would kill her slowly.

"Relax, Jew. I assure you the anatomy lesson will come later. For now, we just have some questions."

"What did you just give me?!" she squeaked.

"Sodium Pentothal. Nonlethal Barbiturate. Painless. Makes it so telling a lie is next to impossible. Now be silent. I'm asking the questions here."

A calming wave washed over to ease Nadir's mind. Suddenly everything felt with her grasp of control, despite knowing the opposite was true. She felt drowsy; too weak to rise from the floor.

"Who are you?"

"Nadir Horowitz," she dozily replied.

"Are you with any military?"

"Yes."

"German military?"

"No."

"American?"

"Yes."

"Where are you from?"

"Munich."

The answer gave Dr. Mengele pause. "And how is it a Jew girl born in Munich came to be in the American service?"

"I made safe passage to Chicago and enlisted once I had citizenship." The quicker Nadir spat an answer, the less she revealed. The serum forced out a reply, but once uttered, no further details felt required. She realized the faster and shorter the answer, the better she could hide the underlying truth.

Dr. Mengele looked to the youths and said, "Now that we have a picture of who our captive is, we'll get down to business." He looked at Nadir and said, "Tell us why you're here?"

"Hunting you," Nadir said. It was the most straightforward and honest answer she could fathom.

"There's no way a thing like you could survive on your own out here. How many others came with you? A dozen?"

"No." She was waging a battle inside her head to concoct a shortcut around the truth.

"More?"

The battle stalemated. "No," she said. She tried to populate her mind with other thoughts. Rafa's sense of humor. The gun. *Those bastards stole Rafa's Browning!* "I want it back!" she blurted.

"Ten?" Dr. Mengele asked, ignoring the outburst.

"No." She couldn't resist. "Give me the gun back! Take the ammo, but please, give it back! It's mine!"

"She's trying to distract herself, class," Dr. Mengele said. "Six?" he asked again.

"Not anymore," she said.

"So then, it's just you and four others?"

"Yes."

"And they're out there looking for us now?"

"Yes."

Dr. Mengele showed a face of worry for the first time in their encounter. "Erick, find *Oberführer* Eichmann and tell him to assemble the council at once."

"Right away, *Reichsmarschall* Mengele," obeyed one of the youths with a straight-armed Nazi salute. He went scuttling out of the chamber.

Dr. Mengele turned his stone-cold gaze back to Nadir and snarled, "How exactly did your team manage to find us? We pay good coin to stay hidden."

"Herman Kline."

Dr. Mengele looked stunned. "You found him? Where?"

"Budapest."

"Is he dead?"

"Yes."

"Careless ingrate," Dr. Mengele muttered. "How well-equipped are your fellow soldiers?"

"Not well at all."

"Machine guns?"

"Just pistols," she said. The room chuckled.

"Do they have any idea what they're looking for? Or that we're out here?"

"No. We only came to investigate. We didn't think we'd find anything except maybe a just few of you," she said.

"Who in the American military do you report to?"

"General Alan Fink."

"And who else?"

"Just him."

"Why such a direct chain of command?"

"We're secret."

Dr. Mengele smiled upon hearing this. "So, you're telling me that if you and your friends were to vanish, essentially nobody would be the wiser?"

Nadir slammed her eyes shut. "Yes," she spilled.

"You see, class? With but a simple interrogation, we've saved the Reich from doom. Now, the council requested I maintain a strict barrier between subject and student, but luckily, the war made me a tad hard of hearing. Do any of you have questions for this rat? This might be your only chance to ever see one in the flesh."

"I have a question, *Reichsmarschall*," a slender, blue-eyed boy of about fourteen said.

"Yes, Gerwin? Go ahead," Dr. Mengele said.

"Jew!" he barked, changing his tone entirely, "How many of your kin did we kill in the great war?"

"All of them," Nadir said. The room erupted laughing.

"Obviously not enough," Gerwin said.

"In due time, Gerwin. Anyone else?" Dr. Mengele said. Another identical-looking boy of slightly older complexion raised his hand.

"Yes, Otto?" Dr. Mengele said.

Otto looked at Nadir with glassy eyes and weakly inquired, "What does Germany look like today?"

"It's bad," Nadir said. "Since the war, Germany has become the world's stage of east versus west. Capitalism against-"

"That's quite enough for today!" Dr. Mengele interrupted. "Rest assured; this won't be our only lesson. But for now, class, we've extracted what we need. We'll break for a long breakfast while I take a meeting, and after, we'll reconvene to discuss our findings. Sound good? Class dismissed."

"Heil Hitler!" the class bellowed with one-armed salutes.

Dr. Mengele stared at Nadir as the youths emptied out of the chamber. The last one out handed him the torch. The swirling flames dancing around his gaunt cheeks cast his face in ominous shadow.

"They're just kids," Nadir said. "They have their whole lives ahead of them. You can't expect to keep them brainwashed in the past forever."

"As if a puny mind like yours could ever grasp what this place is. They're our key to rewriting history." He stared a moment before saying, "We will continue this later. I'll have some food sent down in the meantime. We wouldn't want to experiment on an empty stomach, now would we?"

Dr. Mengele broke into an unsettling whistle as he strolled away. Nadir laid back in the dirt and exhaled, her body still flushed with the effects of the injection. The broken glass remained hidden.

CHAPTER 22

THE *FÜHRER* DESIGNATED their mission top priority. Nazi scholars spent years combing through ancient texts for clues about its fabled location, but finally, in 1939, a secret team dispatched to the jungle. Compared to the resistance their Arian brethren faced in Europe, the primitive Amazonian tribespeople seemed like target practice. After the last resisters were killed, the Nazi archeologists piled the slaughtered dead and burned them in a giant pyre in front of the ancient temple. Then they descended inside, where they were horrified to discover the lowest chamber was filled with sacrificial human remains. They scoured the place for weeks but found no trace of what the *Führer* sought- the legendary Elixir of Life. Their only acquisition to report back would be the liberated real estate.

At first, the expedition was considered a failure. Only in the jaws of defeat did it prove to be the Reich's saving grace. Upon return in '45, the Nazi refugees were pleased to find everything they'd need for a fresh start.

As more Nazis trickled in over the ensuing months, the new Reich slowly took form. The human remains left untouched by the first archeologists were cleared out and tossed into the lake. Teams worked round the clock for weeks to convert the temple into a new Wolf's Lair. Huts were erected around the complex, followed eventually by larger wooden structures. Public works were established, and civilian life flourished. Trees were cleared in the surrounding forests to plant and harvest crops, and finally, massive tent poles with camouflaged nets were erected to conceal their activity from the sky. Once the village breached two hundred, a sense of normalcy resumed.

Now eight years later in the new Wolf's Lair, Dr. Mengele looked around the room at the *Oberführer* council: Adolf Eichmann, Klaus Barbie, Hermann Michael, Gerhard Cuckrus, Walter Weber, and Von Schwangau. All the *Oberführers* held the same rank, just with different responsibilities.

Barbie cleared his throat and said, "I can brush off a mining expedition, sure. But a military outfit of American Jews is cause for concern. Perhaps we should wake him?"

"He needs rest," Dr. Mengele said. "We're entering the final phase, and the Reich needs leadership wellbeing now more than ever. We will not disturb him with a problem we can solve ourselves."

Barbie folded his arms. "It still marks two points of contact with the outside, all within a very short span of time. I, for one, have never been a believer in coincidences."

Eichmann desperately wanted to interject. Instead, he kept his lips pursed. He should have been chosen as the *Führer's* number two. Dr. Mengele was too crafty to be thwarted out of his elevated position as *Reichsmarschall*, and Barbie and Von Schwangau remained locked an ever-at-odds competition that Eichmann saw no value in. If he ever wanted his chance, he had to be smart about it.

"It's sheer bad luck. Nothing more," Dr. Mengele dismissed. "I can't say for certain why an American mining expedition chose here of all places, but the Jews found us through Herman Kline. And according to our prisoner, they'll be scarcely missed once they're eliminated."

"What do they know about us?" Eichmann asked.

"Not a damned thing. The advantage of surprise is still ours, not to mention they're hardly even armed. The prisoner confessed they've got nothing more than handguns. We just have to find them before they can report back."

"I could circle in the fighter," Gerhard offered. "Once I spot them, it's all over." As the only surviving member of the once-fearsome *Luftwaffe*, he thirsted for an opportunity to fly the Reich's only warplane.

Dr. Mengele shook his head. "We can't afford to damage the fighter at this stage. Not over a pest problem."

Weber cleared his throat. "What if I raised the militia?" he suggested. As *Zivil Oberführer*, it was his duty to oversee the Reich's civilian population, which included calling the militia to arms.

Von Schwangau objected, "No. This is something I'd like to contain myself, pending the council's blessing." He looked around the room searching for approval. All except Dr. Mengele nodded.

"Absolutely not," Dr. Mengele said.

Von Schwangau stared unblinkingly through his iron mask.

"I meant no offense," Dr. Mengele corrected. "It's just- if you're injured, or worse, well, do I need to spell it out? There's no one else capable of piloting the U-boat. If we're not risking the fighter, we're certainly not risking you."

Von Schwangau's fists clenched tight. "*Reichsmarschall*, my family hunted game for hundreds of years in the old country, and I'm not talking squealy little pigs. These were monsters with tusks. Compared to what I'm used to, a pack of poorly-armed intruders are nothing. Even if something happened, I've been preparing the youths for quite a long time. I'm as confident in their abilities as I am in my own."

"You of all people should know there is a difference between training and real-time. How can you expect them to get the U-boat all the way out to sea when they've never even taken it around the lake?" Weber said.

"If I may...?" Eichmann voiced as he stood up. "I think these Jews would make a lovely test for our newest *Hitlerjugend*. We've got a dozen lads eager to start night patrols. Why not send a few groups out?"

"Ambushing the miners was one thing. Jews or not- they're still soldiers," Von Schwangau replied.

"They know these woods a hell of a lot better than any intruders ever could. I vote to dispatch a small group of *Hitlerjugend*," Eichmann said.

"Enough bickering," Dr. Mengele injected, "*Oberführer* Von Schwangau, we have the means to take care of this without over-exerting ourselves."

The mask prevented everyone from seeing Von Schwangau's scowl. "Let me illustrate something," he said. "Our youths might know the land, but soldiers know combat. It doesn't matter how well they're equipped. The youths will be grossly outclassed. What do you think might happen if one of them got captured?"

"They'll never talk," Eichmann said.

Von Schwangau folded his arms. "We've trained them as defense scouts, not as spies. It won't just be target practice for the Americans if we dispatch any *Hitlerjugend*. It's handing them our secrets on a silver platter. I'm the only one who can take them out."

Dr. Mengele sighed. "*Oberführer* Eichmann, arm up a squad of our newest *Hitlerjugend*, break them up into groups, and dispatch them for the hunt." He turned to Von Schwangau and said, "*Oberführer* Von Schwangau, if you insist, you may take to the trees as well. Just please be careful."

Gerhard raised an arm. "*Reichsmarschall* Mengele, can I ask what you intend to do with the prisoner?"

Dr. Mengele allowed a twisted smile to form. "I haven't had a good subject in years. There are some procedures I'm dying to experiment with, so rest assured, I will make the most of her. In the meantime, we've also received word from the air. The Russians will be touching down shortly. Eichmann, Von Schwangau, you have your

orders. Everyone else, we'll prepare a welcome party at the runway."
He put up his arm and ended the meeting by saying, "Heil Hitler."

"Heil Hitler," the *Oberführers* repeated.

CHAPTER 23

THE SOUND of a plane's engine jolted Thompson awake. He zipped out of his sleeping hammock and dashed toward the cliff.

Over the hills in the face of the rising sun, he saw the black silhouette of a plane preparing to touch down. "What the hell?" he said to himself. He turned back to his sleeping comrades and hissed, "Guys, get out here. You've got to see this!"

Bar-Yochai joined Thompson at the cliff to watch the plane deploy its landing gear. Herschel caught the tail end before the plane slipped behind the hills.

"What'd I miss?" Vadim asked, sleep still clinging to his sunken eyes.

"A plane landed over there," Thompson said, pointing to the hills. "Looked like a military transport. The question is, whose military, and what's it doing out here?"

Thompson dug the silk map out of his pack.

"What should we do?" Herschel asked.

"We're cutting it damn close for time as is. Luckily that plane landed in the direction we need to go anyway. We'll loop back to the rendezvous, and if Nadir isn't there, we move on and collect as much intelligence as we can before extraction."

"What if we don't find her?" Vadim asked.

Thompson put the map away and shifted uncomfortably.

"Are you really prepared to leave her, Thompson?"

"Vadim, we don't have supplies to last if we miss our ride. We either gather all the intel we can get ourselves out, or we die. If we don't find her, I'll strongarm Fink to get us back here inside of a week. I don't care what it takes."

"But you said getting us out here was the hardest part. How do you propose doing it twice on short notice?"

Thompson frowned. "Enough. Pack up and let's move out." He couldn't mask the defeat trickled within his words.

The cliffs were still slick from rainfall. Twice Thompson's grip slipped. Vadim did most of the climb without daring to look down. For forty tiring minutes, they scaled the ledge back. At the final stretch, the sound of machine gun fire drummed from the direction of the hills.

Thompson held up a hand. They hung suspended over the cliff listening.

A second gunfire volley clapped through the air, this time sequential one-by-ones.

Eerie silence blanketed the valley after the final shot.

Thompson signaled to move on. They collected at the ledge and wiped the dirt from their exhausted hands.

"Any guesses what that could have been?" Herschel said.

All Thompson could do was shake his head.

They quietly marched for two more hours back the direction they'd come the day prior. They reached the rendezvous point with the sun hanging directly overhead. Nadir remained absent.

"Dammit," Vadim muttered.

"We'll replenish and take a little breather," Thompson said. "But this means we have to move on."

They feasted on ration bars and drank their water reserves, then refilled their canteens and splashed off in the river.

"Watch, I'll get attacked by a giant snake," Herschel joked in waist deep water. He cupped his hands and threw water all over his face and body.

"That's not funny," Thompson said.

Everyone stopped what they were doing when they heard footsteps approaching. They all dashed out of the river and hid behind a tree. German voices were next to enter their ears.

"That was weakness, Otto. You can't show them that," Gerwin said.

"She didn't seem so dangerous to me," Otto replied. "And the *Reichsmarshall* seemed troubled by what she had to say."

"We should be so lucky, to be able to go Jew hunting. My father used to tell me about it. They'd shoot them by the dozen back then. Made great sport of it!"

"How's about we make sport out of you two?" Herschel announced in German.

The young Nazis turned around and were greeted by four pistols pointing in their faces.

"Hands up," Herschel said.

Otto raised his hands above his head, letting his MP-40 dangle freely by its neck strap. Gerwin defied, tightly gripping his gun. If he was fast enough, he could let off a bullet spray and kill them all. Then he'd be a hero.

"Kid, you pull that trigger, it's suicide. We've got the drop here," Herschel warned.

Gerwin contemplated. This was life or death.

"One..." Herschel counted.

Otto nudged Gerwin. The Jew was right. He could always pull something once they dropped their guard. He sighed and raised his hands above his head.

Vadim and Bar-Yochai removed their submachine guns and installed them around their own necks.

Herschel looked to Thompson. "Take a seat in the mud," Thompson instructed the boys in German.

"Are you going to kill us?" Gerwin asked.

Thompson first looked to his men, then to the youths. He noticed their camouflage-colored uniforms.

"Ordinarily, we'd have put a few rounds through the backs of your skulls. That's what we do to people who wear those," he said, pointing to their swastikas. "I killed a few your age back in Berlin. Wasn't proud of it, but I did it then, and I'll gladly do it again. Whether you live or die now depends entirely on you two."

"Eat shit, Jew!" Gerwin flouted, spitting on the ground. "Do your worst. You don't scare me."

Thompson raised his 1911. "Is that seriously your answer?"

"Thompson," Vadim chimed. "We should really keep them alive."

"Shoot me! I don't need your rotten sympathy! I'll gladly die with honor right now if that's what it comes to," Gerwin said.

"Thompson, if you pull that trigger, they'll come swarming this way," Vadim said.

"You're lucky my friend can talk sense into me," Thompson said. He looked away and then suddenly clubbed Gerwin over the head with his gun. "I don't like this one. Toss him in the river. Maybe he comes to and swims, maybe he doesn't. We'll put him in God's hands."

Herschel, Vadim, and Bar-Yochai nodded. They hoisted Gerwin up by his arms and legs, trudged into the river, and tossed him in.

Otto dripped terror as he watched his friend float away. Thompson took no pleasure in observing the youth urinate in his pants.

Thunder rattled from the clouds. Herschel, Vadim, and Bar-Yochai returned to Thompson, who had yet to shift his gaze away from Otto.

"Your face is a fucking postcard right now, kid," Herschel taunted. "You should see it."

"What is your name?" Thompson asked.

"Otto..." the boy timidly replied.

"Otto, how old are you?"

"Fifteen."

"Where were you born?"

"Dusseldorf, but my family moved to Frankfurt just before the war."

Thompson observed his trembling hands and placed his own hands over to calm him.

Otto looked puzzled. He had always been told Jews were cold to touch.

"Relax. So long as you don't do anything stupid and answer my questions, this will all be over soon. Now, I don't know if you've noticed, Otto, but this sure as shit isn't Frankfurt. So, what's a blonde-haired, blue-eyed swastika-wearing lad doing so far from home?"

Tears streaked down Otto's face. "I don't remember much about coming over. But this is our new home now. We made it our own!"

"You and who else?"

He shook his head.

"Otto," warned Thompson.

"I can't!"

Thompson and his men exchanged uneasy looks. "Bar, keep an eye on the kid," he said. He nodded for Herschel and Vadim to follow him out of earshot.

Bar-Yochai trained his gun on the youth. He knew the kid would have popped them the first chance he got, but it didn't change things. Killing kids- even Hitler Youth- was a damning affair.

"It sounds like the kid is describing a village," Thompson said. "Every lead we've had since we formed Nesher Unit has pointed to something like this. It would explain how they got an anti-aircraft gun and why so many were coming to South America."

"What should we do with him?" Vadim asked. "He's cooperating. But we can't let him go. He'll go squealing the instant we turn our backs."

"Let's see what else we can get from of him first. We'll decide after that," Thompson said.

They stepped back to see Bar-Yochai wiping blood off of his knife. Otto was dead on the ground with his throat leaking blood.

"What did you do?!" Vadim shrieked.

"Kid made a move for my gun, I swear," Bar-Yochai said.

Thompson stared coldly at his comrade. He'd known him twenty-six years, and the lassitude of Bar-Yochai's usually calm demeanor hinted truth.

"Stupid kid," Thompson mumbled. "Search him and let's toss him in the river. Hopefully, something's hungry down-stream," Thompson said.

They turned Otto's body over and emptied all his pockets. They only found a lighter and a pocket knife. Leaving the contents on the body, they moved him into the water.

CHAPTER 24
SIBERIA - THREE DAYS AGO

A CORPSE DOES NOT ROT in the Siberian wilderness. Submerged by snow, it freezes and will remain hidden for years, even centuries- if it's ever found at all. Such would be the fate of General Petrov Sergeyev. With a fresh gunshot wound to the head, Valentin opened the door and shoved his lifeless body out of the moving truck.

With the General dead, Valentin double-tapped his horn. In unison, gunshots flashed from the cabins of the other six trucks in the caravan. A body fell out of each truck's passenger side to join General Petrov's wintery grave. Moscow would never know what exactly happened on that deserted snowy road- only that a great betrayal had taken place.

The plan required months of planning and a mountain of bribery, but once the weapon was liberated, the caravan headed to the deepest recess of northern Siberia. There, a fully-fueled Tupolev Tu-75 awaited in a remote hangar. They arrived to find all but two men were machine-gunned, betrayed in conjunction with the plot's secrecy.

A mechanical lift delicately extracted the weapon from the truck and loaded it into the plane's belly. Then the traitors fastened it down with chains.

Valentin ignored the action as he smoked a cigarette, staring through the open hangar doors at the Siberian tundra. The blizzard had ceased, and the sun was just peeking through dark clouds to bask the landscape in frozen daylight. The sight brought a tear to Valentin's eyes. He dropped the cigarette and stepped on it knowing this was the last time he'd ever stand on Russian soil.

"This isn't the same home as we grew up in. We had no future here," Alexei said from behind. He had been right to recruit Valentin to join the plot. "You're a dead man walking," he confided one night nearly a year ago. "We both are, and you damn well know it, Valentin. Eventually, it's all going to come crashing down, and I for one will not let a brick wall be the last thing I see before my brains are blown out all over it. I trust this man, Boozis. If he's confident the plan will work, then so am I. We just need your help."

Stalin made the weapon's production and testing a top priority. All Valentin had to do was grease a few palms to divert one to Siberia for a test that would never take place. If anything, General Sergeyev's absence would make him a top suspect, not a victim.

They took off from the hangar without bothering to hide the bodies of those they had betrayed. But even from the air, it all seemed disturbingly easy. They freely flew south over Russian airspace with a payload that carried the power to decimate entire cities. Valentin stayed awake for the entire flight, confident they'd be intercepted and forced to land. But it never happened.

Their first refueling stop was in the northern tip of China. Somewhere over the Mongolian desert, Anton, the Tupelov's pilot, said, "I keep playing this out in my head, and I don't like where it goes." That they were joining escaped Nazis was exemplary to the motherland's dire state of affairs.

Valentin curled his lip to form a snarl. "Anything is better than where we were, Anton. So long as they keep us safe, those Germans can do as they please. Who cares what they do with it? If you ask me, the world needs a fresh start anyway. Setting one of those things off might be the only answer."

"Let's talk this through: They explode it. Someone blames someone else. Then what? You can't save the motherland if there's nothing left after a nuclear war."

"Call me a cynic, but I don't see any other way to save Russia from itself. As for the fallout, we'll be far enough south to withstand anything."

Anton neglected to reply. Valentin sat quietly thinking. "This Jinter Boozis fellow seems to know what he's doing. I've never met him face-to-face, but Alexi has. They've worked together for quite some time. I trust anyone Alexi does."

"But do you trust the Germans?" Anton asked.

"What choice do we have, comrade? It's too late to turn back now." Valentin reached for a bottle of vodka and took a pull.

Jinter arranged all the refueling checkpoints well in advance. After stopping in rural China, they made their way to a secluded airfield in northeast Africa. They refueled one final time at the Horn and then stole clear across the Atlantic Ocean to Brazil. The Tupelov could reach speeds of five-hundred and forty-five kilometers per hour. Given their payload and fourteen-man crew, the plane flew at a sluggish four hundred and sixty. It took all night to reach the Brazilian coast, and another two hours into the dawn to arrive at the jungle stronghold.

The Tupelov came in over an expansive lake glimmering from the rising sun. Along the far shoreline, Valentin spotted an odd collection of structures hidden beneath a network of sprawling camouflage-colored nets suspended by tent poles at least one hundred feet high. Beneath the nets, he could see a massive stone temple surrounded by huts and wooden buildings.

"Get a l-load of this place," Valentin slurred. He'd become intoxicated to the point of sickness after imbibing the remainder of vodka.

"Everyone, strap in. We're touching down," Anton shouted.

A group stood waiting at a dirt runway. A youth was waving them down with landing flags.

God, what has it ever come to? Valentin thought when he saw the landing flags bore black swastikas.

"This is going to be a rough landing," Anton said. He nervously ground his teeth as he disengaged the engines to touch down.

The Tupelov creaked with strain under its immense weight. He could feel the wheels digging into the moist soil. The cabin violently shook, but he managed to glide the beast to a graceful stop right in front of the Nazis.

All hands broke out cheering. Anton flipped a switch and opened up the rear cargo doors. Dr. Mengele, Eichmann, and a dozen MP-40-touting youths awaited outside.

"Trust a Russian to deliver," Dr. Mengele said smiling.

"Trust in Jinter Boozis," Alexi replied in broken German.

Some of the men would have to study up if they were to live together- himself included.

He stepped down the ramp to shake Dr. Mengele's hand. "Nice to meet you. It's a bit hot, but I think we'll come to like it. My name is Alexi, and this is my closest confidant, Valentin. Our pilot, Anton is up there, and the rest of the men you can meet after we get settled. We are very tired and eager to stretch our legs." He stopped to listen to a screeching howl sounding from the jungle. "What is that?"

"The monkeys. They take time to get used to, believe me." Dr. Mengele looked up at a massive wooden crate chained down in the cargo hold and said, "So is that it?"

Alexi grinned. "I must confess, we took turns riding it in the air. Gives you a feeling, knowing you're sitting on all that power."

Dr. Mengele let out a chilling laugh that exterminated Alexi's smile. "Unload the box and do as we spoke," Dr. Mengele instructed the youths. He then looked to Eichmann and nodded approvingly.

"Do we have what we need?" Eichmann asked.

"It certainly appears that way," Dr. Mengele said. "I am very pleased," he added to Alexi.

A few of the youths marched aboard the plane and began cutting the chains with bolt cutters. Others took pose atop the rear cargo doors brandishing their MP-40s, unbeknownst to the Russians on the runway.

"Where will our quarters be?" Valentin asked. "I'm ready to bathe and sleep, I think."

Dr. Mengele pointed to the lake and said, "You'll find all your accommodations out there."

"Very funny," Valentin said. The Russians laughed when he translated it.

"I'm afraid I'm not joking," Dr. Mengele grimaced, plugging his ears as he stepped away.

The youths simultaneously machine-gunned six of the Russians. The remaining eight fell back to back with hands raised high.

Eichmann put up a hand for the youths to hold their fire. They lowered their submachine guns with emotionless stares.

"You can't do this! Mr. Boozis promised us safe passage!" Alexi begged.

"Jinter Boozis is dead, I'm afraid. So is any deal he made with the likes of you," Dr. Mengele said.

"We stabbed Russia in the back for you!"

"Then it's fitting we pay it forward, don't you think?" Eichmann said. "Helga?" he asked a brown-haired teenage girl.

Helga's red-hot MP-40 still simmered as she stepped forward. "Yes, *Oberführer* Eichmann?"

Eichmann undid the strap of his holster. He daintily removed his Lugar, looked it over, and said, "Take this, Helga." Then he looked to the rest of the youths and barked, "Lay them out."

The youths strong-armed the defiant Russians and forced them to their knees. "Helga, shoot these dogs yourself."

"Thank you, *Oberführer* Eichmann!" she gushed. She cocked the weapon and leisurely walked down the line, discharging rounds into the Russians heads. Once she reached the end of the line, she blew off the barrel, ejected the spent magazine, and handed it back to Eichmann.

"Excellent, Helga. Go enjoy a long breakfast in the festivity chambers. You've made me very proud."

The girl Hitler-saluted her *Oberführer* and left grinning. Eichmann secretly hungered for a new young girl to bed and given her prowess, the youth was at the top of his list.

"Marvelous," Dr. Menegle cooed. The youths had cracked open the crate to expose the bomb's shiny metal hull. "It's hard to believe something so destructive could be fit into such a relatively small shell. They'll rue the day they ever brought such a weapon into existence."

Eichmann plugged his nose. The Russians had all defecated their pants. Given that they'd just traveled 15,000 miles to be murdered, such a thing was certainly understandable. "Throw the bodies in the lake," he instructed. "Once that's done, take the weapon to the hangar and load it aboard the U-boat."

"Yes, *Oberführer* Eichmann!" the youths cried.

"Oh, and Pitz?" Eichmann called to one of the youths. Pitz scurried over and saluted. "Yes, *Oberführer* Eichmann?"

"Fetch *Oberführer* Webber and have him assemble the woodworkers. We'll need to construct a hangar for the Luftwaffe's newest acquisition."

"Yes, *Oberführer* Eichmann!" the boy saluted.

CHAPTER 25

THE DUNGEON TEEMED WITH INSECTS, mushrooms, and rats. Nadir shuddered to think what torture Dr. Mengele might concoct should she fall ill from a rodent bite. The Sodium Panthenol left her with a splitting headache, and now she'd completely lost track of time.

Eventually, her stomach growled, subtly at first, then louder and louder until it hurt. A Nazi cadet brought her a plate with mystery meat and vegetables. She hardly trusted their food, but if she allowed herself to starve, she'd never escape. She reluctantly ate the food thinking about the broken glass she had hidden. Surely, she could do *something* with it. *But what?* She closed her eyes to concentrate.

A crawling sensation caused her to squirm. She looked down to observe a large red-and-blue worm wiggling between her toes. Her captors stripped everything except her undershirt and pants. She desperately longed for her shoes back.

She noticed a form stirring in the shadows. She thought it was just her imagination until she squinted. "Hello?" she asked in German. "Is someone there?"

A young boy stepped into the torchlight holding a jug of water. She recognized him from the interrogation. His clammy white skin appeared dotted in sweat. "Is it true?" he breathed in hushed German. He looked back to see if anyone was coming.

"Is what true?" Nadir replied.

The boy inched closer. "That you're a witch?" he whispered. "I can't tell. I've never seen one before."

"Who told you I'm a witch?"

"My father. He said all Jews are dangerous creatures who were created to remind us of darkness and light. That's why we killed so many in the great war."

"If I was a witch, would I really stay locked up?"

He scratched his head. "I guess not."

"Please," she begged, "Let me have some water. I'm so thirsty."

He hesitantly put the jug up to the bars and poured. Nadir fell to her knees drinking. She suddenly felt strong again.

"Now if I was a witch, would I drink water?"

"Maybe not. In the stories I know, witches hate water."

Nadir stood wiping her lips.

"Do your kind have names?" he asked.

"Yes, we're ordinary people just like you. Mine is Nadir. What's yours?"

"Penrod."

"Penrod. That's a lovely German name. Are you supposed to be down here like this, Penrod?"

"No. I could get in big trouble. But I like to sneak around, especially late at night when everyone is sleeping."

"Is it late right now?"

"Very," Penrod said. "But most are awake tonight. I think everyone is afraid of your friends."

Nadir felt a churn in the pit of her stomach. If only she'd been stronger. She could have kept her mouth shut and avoided exposing Nesher unit. Her words had probably inspired a hunting party and doomed them all.

"How far underground are we?" Nadir asked.

"I don't know. The tunnels go up and down," Penrod revealed.

Nadir bustled with questions. "Who dug them?"

"I don't know that either. It was like this when we arrived. Well, not everything. We made changes. Added stuff- The sky net that keeps us hidden and all the buildings around town. But they said in class the excavators found this place just before the great war."

Nadir knew tales of Nazi archeologists scavenging the world in search of ancient treasure. *Perhaps they'd come across this place searching for something else? Or maybe they actually found what they were seeking?*

Then she realized Penrod said "class."

"Penrod," she started. "Um. What did you mean when you said 'class?' Do you have a school here?"

"Well, yeah?" Penrod blankly said. "Didn't you go to a school?"

"Well, yes," Nadir said. "But you have enough kids here to have a school?"

"Sure, until we're fourteen. Then we get special training. We can either become soldiers, or we can join the guilds. Some kids become bakers or woodworkers or fishers. But if we want to be hunters, we have to be soldiers too."

It's a thousand time worse than we imagined, Nadir thought. She tried to conceal her surprise. "How do you stay hidden? If you have a functioning city, you must have had help from the outside, right?"

"I don't know. We learn more about the history when we get older. People come by plane every so often. I don't know who they are, but sometimes they take stuff from the gallery. Other times bad people come. We always get rid of them."

"Gallery? What's that?"

"That's where we keep all the art and stuff from the old country. It's my favorite place to sneak into."

Incredible, Nadir thought. *They're using stolen art to finance it all.*

"If you have all this stuff set up, then how many years have you been here?"

Penrod folded his arms. "I don't think I should say anymore.

They wouldn't like it, and I'm not supposed to be down here. Nice talking to you, um... Nadir. Bye."

"Wait! Hang on a sec! Penrod! What if we played a little game?"

Penrod stopped shy of the doorway. "What sort of game?"

This will never work, Nadir thought. Then she remembered the isolated boy probably wasn't too familiar with old tricks. "A fun one! C'mon, what do you say, Penrod?"

Penrod looked back at the coast. "I don't know. Father wouldn't like me playing games with a Jew."

"He wouldn't like you down here conversing with one in the first place, yet here you are. And look? Nothing bad has happened. Please. I am so very bored. Won't you play a game with me? Just for a little while?"

Penrod huffed. "Okay. But only for a little while. What's the game?"

"Do you like riddles?"

"I guess," Penrod said. She could tell he expected something more thrilling. "What are the rules?"

"Simple. I will tell you a riddle, and if you guess it right, you get to ask me a question. Guess wrong, and I get to ask you one. Sound good?"

"Fine. But if I don't like it, I'm leaving."

"Deal," Nadir grinned. She got right up to the bars and said, "Here we go. First riddle." Rafa loved riddles and instilled them in her from the very first time they met. She'd have to thank him if she ever saw him again. "Okay, I've got one. I'm always thrashing; seldom still. Careful getting in, I'm known to kill. What am I?"

Penrod contemplated and said, "The sea."

"You got it! You're very smart," Nadir gleamed. "Now you can ask me any question you like."

Penrod looked right into her eyes. "If we Arians are the master race, why did we lose the great war?"

Nadir imagined he wasn't allowed to ask such damning truths. "Mistakes were made," she said. "Too many, Penrod. The Allies didn't make them like the Germans did, and that's what turned the tides."

"Like what?"

"Well, Dunkirk Beach, for one."

"What's that?"

"In the spring of '41, Germany had the entire British army pinned against the ocean. But the Germans made the mistake of allowing them to slip away. If they'd been crushed then and there, the entire war might have turned out differently. But that's just one example of many."

Penrod steadily inched closer to the cell bars. "Time for another riddle," he said.

Nadir gripped the bars. "Okay, let me think. Oh, I've got one. Each morning, I lie at your feet. All day I pursue, no matter how fast you run. Nothing can stop me, not even the sun."

Penrod thought a while, looking down at his feet. "Oh!" he cried upon realizing. "It's a shadow!"

"You guessed it," Nadir said. "Ask your question."

"Have you ever killed anyone before?"

"Yes," Nadir replied.

"How many?"

"More than a few."

"How?"

"That's another question. To get the answer, I must ask another riddle, first. Are you ready?"

Penrod nodded.

"What is a box that holds keys with no locks, yet can unbind a person's soul?"

Penrod crinkled his expression and said, "What?"

"What is a box- that holds keys with no locks- and can unbind a person's soul?"

"That's a trick question," Penrod declared.

"No, it's a riddle, and it's not a very hard one if you think about it."

Penrod sat down in the dirt against the bars and pondered. "Box without locks but keys... unbind the soul... I don't know?"

"A piano, silly," she said. "My turn to ask a question."

Nadir had to strategically place these questions as best she could, enough to learn but not so much as to shy Penrod off. The boy could also be whisked away at any moment, destroying any hopes she had.

"What do you remember about coming to this place?" she asked.

"I was young. Maybe four or so." He thought a moment longer before shifting to a melancholic tone, "I still remember home. There was so much rumbling from the bombs, it was like thunder. I remember father coming in through the front door, blood all over, telling us we had to leave. I'll never forget his face. We couldn't even pack. There was a whole line of cars waiting to take us to the harbor. We all boarded a U-boat, and then took the smelliest voyage of my life. We weren't allowed to surface much. It was gross. Eventually, we made it all the way here."

"How many people are living here?"

"That's not how the game works," Penrod protested.

"Sorry, you're right. I need to ask a new riddle. Let's see." She thought for a moment and said, "Say my name, and I disappear. What am I?"

"God," Penrod said.

"Nope," Nadir corrected. "The answer is silence."

"But it's the same thing," Penrod asserted. "I don't believe in God. Say his name. It's words, and then it's nothing but breath in the wind."

Nadir's stared. It was the most intellectual thing she had ever heard from a youth. She nearly deviated into a long philosophical discussion, until she remembered her setting. Her timetable shrunk with each passing moment.

"That's an interesting argument, Penrod, but it's not the correct answer. Now you have to answer one of my questions."

"Father was right. Your kind are tricksters," Penrod fumed, standing up.

Just as he turned to walk away, she said, "Fine, very well. I liked your answer anyways, Penrod. Please come back."

"You do have a God, don't you?" Penrod asked. "Even Jews have gods, I thought. Surely you can't know why I don't believe in one?"

"I can, as a matter of fact. I was like you once, Penrod- A nonbeliever. But that all changed. If you care to keep playing, I'll tell you all about it."

Penrod looked back at the entryway. Nobody was coming, so he turned back and sat right up against the bars. "Okay. Let me hear it. What made you change?"

"I should be long dead, Penrod, but somehow, here I sit. Even getting down to this jail right here- I should be dead twice over."

"You became a believer because you were captured?" Penrod asked.

"No. I became a believer through your kin, actually. Those you call family, Penrod, they've killed nearly everyone I called mine. They've tried and failed on me too many times to count. Now I think maybe, just maybe, everything happened for a reason. That's the way God works."

Penrod looked at her with an expression wholly evil for the first time in their interaction. "Not to be the bearer of bad news, but they might get you this time," he said.

Nadir tried not to break face. "Are you ready for a new riddle?" she asked.

"Sure."

"What has no head, two arms, and no hands?"

Penrod repeated the riddle to himself, eyes squinting to try and figure it out.

"Think about it."

"Shh!" he snapped. "No head. Two arms. No hands. Oh, I've got it. An empty rowboat!"

Nadir smiled. "That's a nice guess, but it's not the answer. It's a shirt, Penrod. A shirt has no head, two arms, but no hands."

Penrod couldn't argue this time. "Ask your question," he fumbled.

"How many people first came here, and how many live here now?"

"The U-boat held forty-eight. Twelve died on the way over, but once we were set up, more and more started coming from the old country. Now there's almost three hundred."

Penrod's answer made Nadir sick to her stomach. Only now did she realize what had swallowed her up. To wait in her cell any longer was a waltz with death. She had to disappear, and fast.

"Next riddle," Penrod said.

Nadir ejected her thoughts and said, "My life measured in hours; I serve by being devoured; thin, I am quick; fat I am slow; wind is my foe."

"Wind is my foe..." Penrod began. "Fat I am slow. Thin I am quick... I serve by being-"

Penrod realized Nadir reached through the bars and grabbed him by the arm. In her free hand, she held a jagged piece of glass to his neck.

"Everything you've been told, Penrod. All of it. Your schooling. Your father's stories. It's all a lie. Listen carefully. They will come for this place soon, and when they do, you have to remember something: You are still very young. You did nothing wrong. Promise me you won't try to fight when they come."

"What are you saying?!" Penrod shouted in a teary, betrayed voice.

"I can't stay locked up here, Penrod. You know what they'll do to me. I'm leaving this cell, and once I'm gone, I'm calling for help."

"No!" Penrod cried.

"It can't be stopped. You might hate me now, but someday, you will thank me. You're too young to realize what's going on here. Just know I am sorry to do this to you. You've shown me incredible kindness." With that, Nadir dropped the shard of glass and wrapped her arm around Penrod's neck. She asphyxiated him through the bars without leaving a mark. It was a knockout technique Uzziel showed her, once upon a time.

She put her finger in front of Penrod's nose to ensure he was still breathing. Then she reached and took off his boots, placing them over her own feet. They fit perfectly. In his back pocket, she found precisely the tool she needed- a metal pen. She disassembled it and set to work picking the cell lock. She would never know the glass she turned into a weapon had been charitably bequeathed by the very person she'd used it against.

CHAPTER 26

THEY FOUND the plane wreckage suspended up in a large nut tree, branches extending like a glove to catch it. From the ground, they could see it was tangled in moss, vines, and spider webs. Gaping bullet holes had been punched through the wings and fuselage.

"That looks like an anti-aircraft gun alright," Herschel commented.

Bar-Yochai said, "This is a different plane. The one we spotted from the cliff made it to the ground."

"Must have been flying pretty low to get hit like that," Vadim said.

"What do you think?" Thompson asked Bar-Yochai.

Bar-Yochai pointed, "First few rounds hit the wing, across the fuselage, all the way like a saw into the other wing. I'm surprised it made it to the tree in one piece."

"Let's get inside and take a peek," Thompson said. He knew this was Bar-Yochai's area of expertise. As a boy, Bar Yochai made it his mission to climb every single tree in Central Park. He succeeded at the age of seventeen without ever once getting stuck.

The nut tree's branches didn't form until twenty feet up. Bar-Yochai first had to scale the surrounding trees, replacing his hands with his feet and going higher with each move as if solving an aerobic puzzle. He reached the fuselage some forty feet up and slipped in through a wide bullet hole.

The wreckage creaked as Bar Yochai climbed inside. He tensed upon finding three skeletons huddled in the rear. Two bodies were adults fruitlessly trying to shield the body of a child. Nature and time had reduced their clothes to weatherworn rags. He averted his eyes before he could drink in the disturbing details for long. He kicked open the hatch and dispatched a rope ladder.

"Will it hold?" Thompson asked from the ground.

"No, I just thought I'd make a joke out of breaking your neck, Thompson. C'mon."

On the ground, an unamused Thompson began to climb through the snickers of Vadim and Herschel. "You two stay here," he commanded.

"You don't have to tell us," Vadim said.

Thompson reached the fuselage and squinted through the vegetation at the bodies.

"Looks like it's been a few years," Bar Yochai said. "We've got two adults. One child. Pilots are nowhere to be seen. Probably got eaten or something."

"This looks like a Beechcraft Bonanza," Thompson said. "Whoever these poor folks were, I bet they sure didn't expect trouble like this."

Bar-Yochai kneeled to rub his fingers along the crusty vegetation growing in a bullet hole. "My thinking, T- we're in an unmarked no-fly zone. I bet if we looked, we'd find a few more wrecks just like this one."

"Let's get out of here," Thompson said.

They climbed down to share their findings. Vadim assembled his camera and snapped a few photos of the plane. "To think, I almost didn't bring this thing," he said as disassembled the camera. "I'm likely to run out of film at this rate."

"Once we're back, I'd like to compile a list of every private plane that's been reported missing within a hundred miles. If we see a spike around a certain year, it might indicate how long they've been hiding," Thompson said. "It could even-"

A steel arrow bolt slammed into the tree inches from Thompson's head. Bar-Yochai tackled him down. A second arrow bolt corrected to impale the wood right where his head was a split-second prior.

"Run!" someone shouted. Thompson didn't even know who said it. The next thing he knew, zinging arrow bolts sailed after them.

They covered over one hundred meters in just a few breaths. Thompson pulled everyone behind a tree to assess and reprieve.

"*Germany!*" a male voice boomed through the trees, "*Awake from your nightmare! Give foreign Jews no place in your Reich!*" The Germanic words seemed to bounce from every direction.

"*We will fight for your resurgence! Aryan blood shall never perish!*" the voice expelled. Then they heard another zing.

"Duck!" Thompson cried.

An impacting arrow bolt sent everyone scurrying back to their feet. The archer was nowhere to be seen, but his voice and onslaught seemed inescapable.

"*All these hypocrites, we throw them out! Judea, leave our German house! If the native soil is clean and pure, we united and happy will be!*"

Wind and branches whipped, cut, and dirtied their faces as they retreated. Another arrow bolt shot right past their heads and stabbed into a tree. Mid-stride, Thompson undid his holster to take out his 1911.

"*We are the fighters of the N.S.D.A.P. True Germans in heart, in battles firm and tough! To the Swastika, devoted are We! Heil our Leader, Heil Hitler to thee!*"

Thompson turned back to steal a glance. A slender masked man draped in a camouflage hunting cloak loaded a fresh arrow bolt from his quiver into his crossbow.

"Keep running!" Thompson yelled. He raised his 1911 and unloaded every bullet he had.

The hunt had only just begun, and Von Schwangau was already considering it the best of his life. He undauntingly aimed as .45 caliber bullets whizzed past his body. He'd never hunted game that was armed before. He calmly squeezed the trigger to launch an arrow at the shooter.

The arrow bolt shot past Thompson's crossfire and darted toward his heart. Just before finding its fatal mark, Thompson squeezed off one final bullet. With mere milliseconds to spare, the heavy .45-caliber lead impacted the arrow bolt head-on and shattered it.

Thompson heard the ricochet and realized in awe what had happened.

The figure paused to reload his crossbow. Thompson considered dueling until he heard Bar-Yochai call his name. He turned and fled, ejecting his spent magazine for a reload as he ran.

Another bolt came shrilling down through the trees. Everyone dove in different directions as it stabbed into the moist dirt.

"Go!" Thompson cried, pulling Vadim to his feet. He ripped the arrow bolt out of the soil and then dashed after.

They raced up a steep incline and lost their footing on the descent. They tumbled down the hill, collecting in a wounded pile at the base of a tree.

"We're done for," Vadim squeaked through grit teeth. He figured he'd just bruised every inch of his body in the fall.

"In here!" Bar-Yochai exclaimed. He pointed to an opening in the earth hidden beneath exposed roots of a dead rubber tree. He slipped in and extended a hand. One by one, they climbed into the mouth of a hidden cave. They backed deep inside with their guns uniformly pointed at the mouth. Their hearts were thundering so loudly in their chests they could hardly hear anything else.

"The second he peers in," Thompson whispered, "fire everything you've got."

Nobody moved a muscle for some time. Thompson broke the long silence by tucking his 1911 away. "I think we lost him."

"He was hunting for us," Herschel said. "They know we're here."

Thompson fished a flashlight out of his pack and shined it on the arrow bolt. The head had a swastika engrained on the tip. "Look at this thing," Thompson said. "Balanced steel. Custom engraving. It's well made."

"I hate to say it, but if the *Shtik drek* in the mask could find us, he could have just as easily found Nadir."

Silence hung for a moment as Thompson continued examining the bolt. "Let's stay hidden for a while. I need a breather after that."

CHAPTER 27

PENROD WAS in for a harsh awakening. Nadir stripped him bare, stole his clothes, stuffed his socks down his throat, and left him hog-tied in the cell. She'd deceived him and made a sham of his pity. She hoped one day he'd see it was for his own good.

Nadir crept through narrow passageways sparsely lit with torches. She stopped when she heard voices echoing ahead.

Two men spotted her at the end of the tunnel. They only paid a momentary glance before disappearing through a chamber to their right.

She continued. Despite the cool subterranean air, she dripped anxious sweat.

The tunnel inclined upward, leveling out at the very last torch. She stepped through an opening and looked straight up at the starry night sky overhead. There was a makeshift ladder built into the twenty-foot-deep hole. She placed her hands on the cold metal bars and climbed up.

She poked her head above ground. The surface looked very different from what she imagined. Much of the sky above was visible through a tiny gap in the thin translucent nets stretching over the entire encampment.

"Genius," she muttered, looking at the nets. From the sky, Nadir was certain nobody could ever spot the village. A token few torches flickered about the perimeter, but mostly it was dark. She observed many wooden buildings and crude huts standing around the ancient complex she had just escaped.

She knew it wouldn't be long until Penrod stirred awake. It would take a while for him to get free, but once he managed to get the socks out of his throat, he could easily call for help.

Instinct demanded she run for the trees, but duty prevailed above all else. If she could learn just a little bit more about who was hiding here, the intelligence could serve to orchestrate a much more significant intervention, one Nesher Unit could never do alone. She needed to get her hands on a gun and fast. Without, she was a defenseless fawn in a den of lions.

Nadir skulked in the shadows, trotting from building to building. Some appeared well-constructed using complex carpentry techniques, while others were minimalist shacks. She imagined the poorly-constructed huts were the first structures erected when the group settled. They'd clearly purchased supplies along the way, for the tools required to construct the wooden buildings were well beyond reach.

"Psst!"

Nadir froze. She turned around to see a dark figure standing against one of the buildings.

"Where's your group?" a male voice asked her in German.

"Where's yours?!" she hissed back. "And what are you doing out here alone?!" She'd played this game before during the war. She learned fast that the easiest way out of a situation like this was to grab it by the horns and seize control.

"Do you not realize? It's *Unterstumführer* Rolf!" the male snapped.

"Quit joking," Nadir teased. "Come here."

"Who is that?" Rolf asked again, stepping closer. "Clovis, is that you?"

"Rolf!" she excitedly said. The lad walked right up, and Nadir punched him square in the nose. He staggered back and shouted, "You hit me! Why-"

Nadir tackled him and bashed his head against the ground. She kicked him in the testicles for good measure and then slipped his MP-40 off of his neck. She dragged the unconscious young Nazi into a narrow gap between two buildings. There she left him flat on the dirt. She squeezed out of the gap donning his MP-40.

Nadir took just a few steps before her ears perked up. From an open window lit by candlelight, she could hear a familiar whistle chirping a fun little melody.

She crept up to the building. Its stocky wooden front doors bore a large red cross.

A medical building. Only a doctor could be in there, Nadir thought.

CHAPTER 28

WE CAN'T EVEN STOP *for sleep,* Thompson thought. They crept back-to-back for at least a mile listening for the whistle of an oncoming arrow bolt. The attack left them harboring a nuanced feeling like prey stuck in a hunter's crosshairs. A sudden mid-day downpour did little to calm their nerves.

"I think we've put safe distance from the cave," Thompson said when they reached a clearing some three hours later. Acres of trees vacated to allow a sea of high grass dominion over the field.

"It'll be getting dark soon," Vadim said. "How do you propose we camp?"

"We can't," Thompson said. "There's no place safe."

"We have two days til' extraction. We can't go that long without sleep. Not in this condition."

Thompson gazed around sheepishly as if hiding something.

"What is it?" Vadim asked.

"Open your medical bag. I might have packed something special when you weren't looking."

"Like what?" Vadim asked. Thompson stayed quiet. Vadim dropped his backpack and extracted his medical pack. "What am I looking for?" he asked, nosing around the bag. He stopped upon reaching a small glass bottle labeled "Pervitin."

"Oh, come on, Thompson. You can't be serious?" He opened the bottle as if expecting it to be a joke. Inside he counted a dozen tablets.

"We sleep, we die. That's the game we're playing now."

"What's in the bottle?" Bar-Yochai asked.

"Thompson, you never consulted me," Vadim said over Bar-Yochai.

"That's because if I wanted a lecture, I would have called my mother. I had a feeling it would come in handy, so I took extra precaution. Give me that bottle."

"Will someone tell me what the hell that stuff is?" Bar-Yochai asked again.

"Amphetamine speed tablets," Vadim said. "It's the same stuff Hitler fed his troops to keep them working."

"I really thought a guy like you would appreciate the irony," Thompson said. He stole the bottle from Vadim and dumped a tablet into his palm. "It's fine. I'll go first." He held the tablet in front of his mouth.

Vadim slapped the pill out of his fingers. "No way. That stuff could kill you in this heat."

"Vadim, I appreciate your concern. But in case you haven't paid attention, our options are nil." Thompson picked the tablet out of the soil and broke it into shards. "We'll compromise. Small amounts, just enough to stay alert."

"We?" said Vadim. "You're not poisoning us all. At least not me."

"Then you're going to be very tired soon because we're not stopping until we're out of here," Thompson said.

Herschel dipped into Thompson's palm and then swashed his Pervitin-coated fingers around his mouth. "Tastes kind of sugary."

"That's what they coat it with," Vadim fumed. "Did I mention how addictive that shit is?"

Bar-Yochai dipped his fingers into Thompson's palm next. "Bar," Vadim said disapprovingly.

"Better a heart attack than an arrow through it," Bar-Yochai said, rubbing his fingers around his gums.

Thompson licked his palm then offered the final remains to Vadim.

"This is such a bad idea," Vadim nagged. He copied procedure dipping his fingers in Thompson's palm and swishing the Pervitin shards around his gums.

"You'll thank me later," Thompson said.

"Yeah, right," Vadim said.

Herschel was the first one to feel the drug's effects. After half an hour of pacing, he noticed it wasn't just the heat- his heart beat much faster. Then his stomach growled so loudly, he physically keeled over. "Oh, dear God," he moaned, clutching his stomach. He descended into a tirade of Hebrew and English swear words as he scurried into the bushes. Everyone grimaced. Herschel groaning as the sound of splashing diarrhea serenaded their ears.

"What's happening to him?" Bar-Yochai asked Vadim.

"Pervitin gives you the shits. Watch, we'll all be like that very soon," Vadim said bitterly.

Two painful hours later, after everyone's bowels evacuated and they'd rehydrated and re-nourished, the amphetamine's properties surged through their bodies. Every sound of the jungle could be scrutinized with high-wired intensity. Their very thoughts were on fire, neurons racing through their minds at light speed. Sleep was the last thing on anyone's mind.

"I want more," Herschel said when the sky started fading dark.

"Shortly," Thompson said. Deep down he feared Vadim might have been right. His body felt so strained, he could hardly imagine two more days of doping. But around dusk, as the effects were waning, his pounding head felt like it was going to split wide open if he deprived himself any longer.

They soon reached another high grass clearing. Vadim took out the Pervitin bottle in the middle of the field and dumped a single tablet into Thompson's palm.

Thompson started to crush it up. Then he stopped. German-speaking voices were approaching.

Thompson looked to his men urgently. At once, everyone dipped into his palm and loaded their fingers with Pervitin.

Thompson licked his palm clean and took out his 1911. They gently rose in unison to peer above the high grass. A dozen armed youths entered the opposite side of the clearing.

"I count twelve," Bar-Yochai murmured. "They're coming right this way."

"Looks like they're just kids," Vadim whispered.

"That doesn't mean they won't kill us. You're welcome to go introduce yourself if you like," Thompson said. "Is anyone else at a moral crossroads?"

Bar-Yochai and Herschel's faces were flat.

"Didn't think so," Thompson said.

"If we move to the trees, we might be able to avoid them," Vadim said.

"Fuck that. Let's take one alive and pop off the rest. Fried fucking sauerkraut," Herschel said. Pervitin fired his eyes with mania.

"Bad move," Bar-Yochai whispered. "That we've made it this far with no further contact was a miracle. Let's not chance our luck just before dark."

Herschel scowled. "We need their weapons, Thompson."

Thompson frowned. "He's right. We need better arms. Prepare to engage. Spread out. Two on each side. I'll throw a stone. Once it hits the ground, we pop up and ambush them. Try to leave one alive."

Thompson and Bar-Yochai took the left flank. Herschel and Vadim took the right. They fanned out twenty feet apart and crept low in the grass.

Vadim grimaced upon hearing just how fast his heart hammered. His hands were shaking, yet he'd never felt such iron confidence before. He felt like his heart might explode out of his chest at any given moment.

With Gerwin and Otto missing, the *Hitlerjugend* in its entirety dispatched in squads of a dozen. Siegfried still boiled bitterly about his Jew bite. He had to get a shot in the infirmary that rendered his entire arm numb. It was hideously embarrassing. He longed to make *Rottenführer*, and in two short years, he'd be eligible. Soldiering through his injury to kill the intruders would be a feat not quickly overlooked. Perhaps one day, Siegfried could even become the next *Führer*.

He glanced to see a stone flying through the air. "Hey!" he called to the group, pointing at the stone.

A dozen submachine guns pointed to track the stone. Just as they heard it impact the ground, gunfire screamed from all around them.

Siegfried was the only one left standing when the guns fell silent. The smell of blood wallowed in the air. Everyone around him was dead. Then he realized the four Jews were boxing him in with guns pointed at his head.

"Look at that. We didn't even wing him," Thompson said in German. "It's your lucky day."

Siegfried's whimpers were muffled by Bar-Yochai's hand grabbing hold of his face. When he tried to bite, Bar-Yochai squeezed so hard, he thought his jaw might pop off.

"Try that again, kid, and I'll rip it clean off your face," Bar-Yochai said. He threw Siegfried to the ground and kneeled to stare. "Now you're going to answer some questions for us."

The Jew's deep green eyes were the most terrifying sight Siegfried had ever known. These were no men- the *Oberführer* council's stories were true. These were *demons*.

"What is your name?" the demon asked.

"S-Siegfried. Please. D-don't hurt me."

"I'm sorry, did we shoot you?"

"N-no," he sniveled.

"What about your hand. What happened there?"

"I was bitten."

"Bitten? By what?"

"Your friend."

Frantic expressions besieged the demons' faces.

"Come again?" Bar-Yochai asked.

"Your friend, the girl!" Siegfried cried. "*Reichsmarshall* had us watch as he interrogated her. She bit me."

Thompson shoved Bar-Yochai aside and plucked the boy right off the ground. "What did you do to her?!" he roared.

"Nothing!" Siegfried managed through eyes spewing tears. "I'm telling you! We gave her truth serum. That's how we knew you were here! Far as I know, she's still alive in the village."

Thompson smiled and dropped Siegfried. "That's a good lad. Tell us more about this village."

Siegfried screwed up his face. *It hadn't occurred to him they didn't know.* His shot at *Rottenführer* shrunk by the second. Another sentence, no, *another sound* more, and Siegfried might as well be committing treason. Surely someone must have heard all those gunshots. All Siegfried had to do was keep his mouth shut and buy time.

Bar-Yochai thumbed back the hammer on his Beretta. "I am going to count to three, kid. One... Two..."

"Bar," Thompson said. "You already stabbed one in the neck. You're not executing another."

"How old are you?" Bar-Yochai asked.

"Fourteen," Siegfried said.

"He's old enough," Bar-Yochai said to Thompson.

"He's just following orders," Vadim said.

"Yeah? In case you forgot, so were the rest of 'em- 'Just following orders.'" Bar-Yochai held his Beretta to Siegfried's head. "We can't let him go. He'll call for backup."

"I've got a better idea," Thompson said. He pointed his 1911 at Siegfried. "We don't give a shit how old you are, Siegfried. You wear one of those Swastikas, we'll shoot you all the same. Just like your kind did to us."

Just a little longer, Siegfried thought.

"I'm not going to kill you. I don't like the idea of it. But I am going to hurt you. Badly." Thompson stuck the gun against Siegfried's kneecap. "Strip those bodies of their guns and ammo. Siegfried and I are going to have a little chat."

Herschel, Bar-Yochai, and Vadim set to work liberating the dead of their MP-40s and spare ammunition.

Thompson leaned close to Siegfried and said, "Now I can put four or five bullets in you before you pass out from the pain. I won't get into how I know that, but trust me, it's a fact. I am going to ask a question, Siegfried. Every time you don't answer, you get a bullet. First question. Where is the village?"

Siegfried pointed west without even considering. "Wrong answer," Thompson said, taking the gun off his knee to point it lower. He squeezed the trigger and fired a shot straight through Siegfried's foot. "One," he counted.

Siegfried cried out in pain. "I told you!"

"No, you lied. Do not test me." He placed the gun back over Siegfried's kneecap. "One more time. Where is the village?"

Siegfried pointed east this time.

"Look at me," Thompson said. He stared deeply into his aquamarine eyes. "Okay, that's more like it." Without warning, he clubbed Siegfried over the head.

"Leave him. We're getting Nadir back tonight.

CHAPTER 29

APRIL 1945 - THE NORTH SEA

AT AGE 32, with over 200,000 tons of enemy cargo sunk, *Kapitän* Kurtz Von Schwangau was the spitting image of the Wolves of the Third Reich. He imagined after the war Germany would hail him as a hero. He loved the Nazi party, and he loved his U-boat crew like they were his children. But one by one, his fellow Wolf *Kapitäns* were sunk. Soon, everyone was gone except for him. By that point, any mission given to him by the imbeciles on shore was certain to get him and his crew all killed. Germany would need its best and brightest if ever to rise from the ashes.

"Where do we go now, *Kapitän?*" one of his sailors asked in the looming face of defeat. But fate was listening in those cold North Sea depths. Von Schwangau couldn't even fathom a reply before his *Kapitänleutnant* interrupted.

"*Kapitän!* We've just received orders from Berlin," the *Kapitän-leutnant* exclaimed, handing Von Schwangau a slip of paper.

Von Schwangau read it a dozen times, hope growing in his eyes upon each pass.

"Activate all engines. We make for port in Cuxhaven," Von Schwangau ordered.

The path to northern Germany was riddled with peril. A depth charge nearly sunk them when they passed under an Allied destroyer. The shock from the blast tossed everyone aboard like rag dolls. Some were impaled on the U-boat's unforgiving steel innards. Four more broke bones in places no remedy could easily cure. A pressure valve also blew right near Von Schwangau's head. Scalding hot steam erupted to sear all the flesh off of his face. The men dressed his wounds, but he knew his comely days would be a distant memory.

The crescent moon shined brightly against the harbor's tranquil black waters. The U-boat's conning tower slithered out of the depths to cut the reflection in two. A group of thirty-nine people- men, women, and children- all stood shivering at the end of a long dock. They weren't trembling from the frigid weather. They'd all just escaped capture and were preparing to embark on a long and dangerous voyage.

The U-boat cut its quiet engines as it crept up to the dock. The waters were a bit shallow for Von Schwangau's liking. Ordinarily, he'd never risk beaching the U-boat like this. But if the orders were correct, the risk was worth the reward.

Von Schwangau emerged from the conning tower donning a Nazi salute. He looked down at the crowd gathered on the dock. All but one saluted back. The man hiding beneath a black SS military cap calmly threw up a dismissive, trembling hand, and then cradled his arms back together.

Von Schwangau could readily observe from the conning tower the *Führer*'s Parkinson's was spiraling out of control. He'd never met the man, yet now he'd been charged with saving his life. He'd do whatever he could to make his king comfortable. "I'm *Kapitän* Kurtz Von Schwangau, and I am very pleased to be welcoming everyone aboard," he explained. "We've had some difficulties getting here. Some aboard are badly injured. I don't know how we're all going to fit, but we'll make it work."

He dispatched a rope ladder down to the dock. The man he

recognized as Adolf Eichmann climbed up first. *"Kapitän,* the *Führer* has charged me with running this evacuation. Look, you have no idea what kind of arrangements we've made. If I might be frank, we'd selected *Kapitän* Topp for this mission but were unable to make contact. Your sick and injured will have to stay here to make room for the rest of the passengers. We're sailing for Norway first. We've arranged repairs for the long voyage ahead."

"Voyage?" Von Schwangau asked. "Where are we going?"

"Kapitän, listen very carefully. Right now, you are all that stands to preserve the Reich from the Allies. The world thinks us dead. Once we go far, far away, we can tally losses and prepare for a new dawn. Until then, the only thing you should know is haste. Understood?"

Von Schwangau couldn't believe his ears. He knew Eichmann to be crafty, but this seemed ludicrous. There wasn't any chance in hell they could sail away in a giant vessel with the *Führer* on board. *Where would they go? How would they live?*

"Herr Eichmann, sir-"

"Kapitän, there isn't time! Evacuate your sick and injured to the dock at once!"

Von Schwangau climbed back into the U-boat to tell the men. Of his thirty-three-man crew, only eight were allowed to stay. The rest begrudgingly unloaded onto the dock to make room. It broke his heart. He knew this wasn't the way his men envisioned ending their wartime service.

He helped load the U-boat with its new occupants, the delicate *Führer* first, then his most trusted command, Dr. Mengele, Herman Michael, and even Klaus Barbie with his entire family. "Daddy, where is Uncle Hitler taking us?" he heard one of Barbie's young children ask.

"On a sea trip!" the Butcher of Lyon joyfully replied.

With everyone safely aboard, Eichmann turned to Von Schwangau and said, "Best you load up. I'll instruct the injured what to do from here."

Von Schwangau saluted his men goodbye. Once inside the U-boat, he heard the rattle of machine gun fire.

Eichmann climbed down and said to him, "Away we go."

"You shot them," Von Schwangau said, dumbfounded.

"*Kapitän*- again, if that is ever going to work, nobody- and I mean *nobody* can jeopardize that. Their sacrifice will be written in our history books when we retake the world. Do we have a problem?"

"No," Von Schwangau feebly replied. Although he never pulled the trigger that fateful night, he always felt his men's blood permanently stained his hands. In the ensuing years, he never told the rest of the crew what happened. He just couldn't bear to.

It didn't take long to arrive in Norway. How Eichmann arranged a secret crew to repair the U-boat was nothing short of remarkable. Even more ludicrous was the giant cache of priceless antiquities waiting for them upon arrival. All able-bodied hands dispatched to load up the U-boat. Von Schwangau needed no subtitles to know this was how they'd be financing operations going forward, wherever they were heading. They had so much plunder, they had to remove all the torpedoes just to utilize the extra space in the tubes. He watched with amazement as priceless works of art were jammed inside.

As the U-boat underwent repairs, Von Schwangau's facial wounds were dressed. He applied an ointment with a fresh bandage wrapping. He'd have to change the wraps and reapply medicine daily for many months to keep it from infection.

Thirty-six hours after docking in Norway, the U-boat was ready to sail. This time Eichmann made no secret of machine-gunning the witnesses. He left the repair crew a gory mess of blood and bullets. Von Schwangau didn't like deceit, but this time he understood. He helped Eichmann set fire to the hangar before embarking.

They traveled at just four knots, surfacing for the first time somewhere near the Faroe Islands. An Allied warship came close to spotting them, but Von Schwangau nimbly managed to slip away. The rules were firm afterward: thirty-three hours submerged, one hour above, and only at night. This was how the rest of the voyage would go.

By the second week at sea, sickness ravaged the U-boat inhabitants. Each time they surfaced, a new body had to be dumped overboard. That everyone didn't die proved destiny offered the Reich another chance.

They were spotted again at the coast of Brazil. Von Schwangau had been through far too much to lose it all to the likes of some lowly fisher. Bringing him down as he boated away was nothing compared to the difficulty they would face on the final part of the voyage.

The Amazon river proved the most treacherous body of water Von Schwangau had ever navigated. He feared they'd get stuck or worse, encounter a waterfall. They'd have to abandon the U-boat if anything went wrong. But fate remained on their side. The U-boat made it upriver all the way into the lake without ever once being sighted. Over the ensuing eight years, the seeds of the new Reich took root, all thanks to Kurtz Von Schwangau.

V on Schwangau removed his iron mask. The U-boat accident destroyed most of the nerves and sweat glands, leaving his face continually feeling numb. He examined the mask and rubbed his finger along a tiny new dent where the Jew had nicked it with a .45-caliber bullet. "Impressive," he said to himself. If it had not been for the mask, that bullet might have killed him.

He turned the mask over and extracted a vial of ointment from his pocket. He unscrewed the vial and poured the ointment in his hands. Using two fingers, he lubed up the mask where his bare wilted flesh touched its surface. Then he applied some to his pink skin.

He hungered to resume tracking the intruders. Ever since leaving his sea legs behind, Von Schwangau had become an avid game hunter, just like his ancestors. He wondered what he'd do with the bodies once he killed them all. *Would he leave them to rot, or have them stuffed like trophies?*

He put his mask back on and set off. Shortly after, gunfire rattled nearby. "There you are," he said, smiling. He loaded a fresh arrow bolt into his crossbow.

THE *FÜHRER* himself delegated *Luftwaffe* ace pilot Gerhard Cuckrus to help envision a world after Germany won the war. At Gerhard's direction, someday every person on earth would have their own flying machine. To him, the sky truly was the limit. *Maybe, eventually, even the moon?*

But then the skies came crashing down. The *Führer's* visionary committee suddenly found itself charged as the rebirth committee. Once defeat looked imminent, the committee put the plan into action.

The *Führer* spent fabulous sums dispatching secret expeditions all across the globe. When it came time to evacuate Germany, Gerhard keenly reminded his superiors of their hidden jungle acquisition. Word spread amongst the hierarchy, but the allies moved swiftly once the backbone of the German army crumbled. Eventually, escape became a free-for-all. Those left behind were captured and hanged.

In May 1945, Gerhard came tearing into an air hangar outside of Berlin in a bullet-ravaged Mercedes Benz Cyprus. He bled freely, but he didn't bother to check where from. Escape was the only thing that mattered.

Bombs dropping near and far sent bits of dust falling from the sprawling hangar ceiling. Gerhard limped out of the Mercedes with a Kongsberg Colt in hand. The hangar housed a single FW-190 with a big swastika decal painted on the tail fin. He didn't time to peel the sticker off. He didn't know how much fuel the fighter had, nor did he have time to gas it. He had to get it airborne. He hobbled into the cockpit, started the engine and quickly took flight. In no time, he circled high above smoldering Berlin.

The higher the plane climbed, the bigger a coward he felt. *This wasn't defeat. It was a test-* a challenge he and the rest of the surviving high command would meet to fulfill humanity's greatest prophecy.

Gerhard left the fighter abandoned in a field in Northern Italy. He'd long shed his *Luftwaffe* uniform, but his bloodied complexion left much to ponder should anyone come across him.

He fortunately encountered Axis sympathizers who gladly provided shelter. Once recovered from his injuries, he continued his journey south all the way to Egypt. From there, he snuck aboard a commercial ship bound for Central America.

Stepping onto the other side of the world, Gerhard felt confident, until he realized he was in British Guiana. He noticed his face sprawled on wanted posters all over the city. He knew every allied personnel would have memorized his face, and minus a change of clothes, he'd done little to alter his appearance.

He couldn't linger. He had to get to the jungle and fast. Every day that went by, his notoriety as an escaped war criminal grew. He had the coordinates. He just needed a set of wings. But with no money and nothing more a single handgun deep inside British territory, it would be an audacious move at best.

He pickpocketed his way around a busy market to earn a few bucks, then searched for taxi drivers until he found one who could speak French like him. He didn't dare use German. He asked the driver for a ride to a nearby military airfield and got dropped off just outside the perimeter fence. He spent an hour casing the place after dark. He surprisingly discovered it lacked much security. It seemed in all their audacity, the British didn't fathom they'd ever be robbed of a plane.

Gerhard easily slipped over the fence to find an unguarded hangar with a lone P-39 Fighter plane stashed inside. He quietly peeled open the hangar doors, one at a time, and then climbed into the cockpit.

The P-39 was fully fueled and armed. The only thing missing was Gerhard's name inscribed in the cockpit. By the time the Brits heard the plane start, he was already pulling out of the hangar. Gunfire pinged the plane, but nothing could stop him once its propellers were spinning. Gerhard was three miles up in the sky before the Brits knew what hit them.

Gerhard memorized those sacred coordinates from the very first communication wires. He knew one day, just maybe, the information might save his life.

He flew all through the night into daybreak. The jungle beneath him was a never-ending wash of shrubbery that stretched endlessly. He grew nervous when his fuel gauge hovered near empty. Just when the plane started to falter, Gerhard reached a vast Amazonian lake. He could see the ancient stone temple protruding from the jungle on the far opposite shore.

Small dots gathered near the temple to watch him fly in. Gerhard ecstatically recognized the specks on the ground as his surviving kin. He had been to hell and back to return to his people, and the once fearsome *Luftwaffe* again had an officer and a warbird in its ranks.

CHAPTER 31

HE COULD STILL HEAR those cheering crowds like it was yesterday. White German faces extending for miles upon miles, all with their right arms triumphantly extended. It was a nation's pride the likes of which Hindenburg and his Weimar weaklings couldn't have conjured in their wildest dreams. They were the descendants of Atlantis. World Ice Theory proved it, and mercy be damned upon the rest of the nations for encroaching on mother Germany's vocation. Those fools could never comprehend what the *Ahnenerbe's* minds proved through years worth of research and expeditions. It was a fact: the globe belonged to the Arians. It was a dream so close he could taste it. He'd never felt so alive as he used to standing before a crowd, professing the future of their destiny.

He saw defeat in his visions, only he didn't dare tell another soul. He was a superstitious man privy to strange things. He truly believed even the slightest utterance would dispel Germany's holy ascent. He wrote the visions off as side effects from the medication, despite however real it felt. *Damn those doctors for prescribing the stuff.*

It started off with small doses, but his failing health and mounting stress from the war effort demanded an ever-increasing prescription. It rendered him a walking medical phenomenon. For over a decade, he'd been routinely taking every drug substance known to man, from psychedelics to barbiturates. And over ensuing years, the Reich's stockpile of special narcotics began to dwindle. Until the jeweler in Budapest entered the picture in '49, any contact with the outside world posed the highest jeopardy.

Only in desperation did he dispatch Mengele and the Reich's three other physicians to scour the surrounding tropics for some kind of substitute. It took a few months, but eventually, they came across a rare and delicate flower that only bloomed two days per year. Its pollen, once concentrated and smoked, yielded incredible medical properties. His Parkinsons tremors temporarily ceased, and somehow his lungs cleared up too. But the flower would render him severely impaired, and too often, he'd suffer terrible hallucinations. But to him, after dosing for generations, anything was better than suffering, and so he chose substance over sanity. He even promoted Mengele to *Reichsmarshall* out of sheer gratitude for the discovery.

He could hear thunder rumbling outside, but down in his spider hole, he felt cozy. He sipped on herbal tea and stared at a freshly packed pipe full of pollen extract. The old medicines administered by his wartime doctors were potent, long-lasting, and riddled with tainting side-effects. This substance was far milder. One puff from his glass pipe would yield a dizzying hallucination for a short period, followed by a calm that lasted for hours.

He took the glass pipe, drew a match, and cast the bright yellow pollen aflame in the bowl. He breathed and toyed with the glass pipe's choke. The pipe had been the first thing the new Reich's gaffer fashioned once his shop was operational.

He coughed and spat smoke everywhere, his eyes rolling back in his head as he fell flat against the mattress. A cloud of smoke danced around his wrinkled face. The thunder outside turned to a roaring crowd inside his head. He closed his eyes.

He was back at the Olympic games in '36, watching from his grand pavilion. Below, his athletes looked so strong as they proudly saluted him. He knew this would be an unforgettable day both for him and for his people.

And it was, in a way he never saw coming. That was the day racial impurity besmirched his beloved home. *But how?* The expression he made that hot August afternoon was alien to his facial vocabulary.

A shadow blacker than the athlete who preluded Germany's disaster gathered in the far corner of the spider hole. It pooled into a mass that manifested and took flight as a tiny eagle.

He laid back dazzled. The bird spread its wings and turned from black to gold as it glided around the tiny confined space. He stared up at the eagle doing circles overhead. He could still hear the Olympic crowd screaming in shock.

The eagle first looked up, then it spun its head all the way around to look down at him.

This was a hallucination so electrifying and scary, his tremors raged through the medication. The eagle bore a human face spliced with a composition of every monster he knew: Golem; Vampire; Witch; Werewolf; Undead; Troll; Ghost... *Jew.* The *Führer* screamed.

CHAPTER 32

AT THE END of a person's life, all they have to show for it is their work. And how proud Dr. Josef Mengele was of his. In twenty years, he'd gone from unknown medical student to the *Führer's* personal caregiver to second-in-command of the new Reich. Perhaps one day soon, the world would recognize his brilliance.

He brooded over an old notebook and thought back to the lives lost creating its pages. He would have done it a thousand times over, even for just a fraction of the results. Science is a field for learning, and *oh, had he learned*.

When they first arrived in the jungle, Dr. Mengele sorely missed his laboratory resources. But he fast grew accustomed to the new Reich's off-the-grid lifestyle. There was something pleasant about it, even in the harsh rainforest climate.

Although he enjoyed the title *Reichsmarschall*, he still preferred "doctor." Everyone in the high council had their own facility in the village, and Dr. Mengele's was, unsurprisingly, the medical building. He sat in an examination room, turning the pages of his notebook with a glass of wine over candlelight. A wicked smile crept across his face as he came across a passage regarding a pregnant woman and the grotesque procedure he performed. He couldn't absorb his savage handwritten account for long. A disturbance caught his attention at the doorway. He looked up to see a figure standing in the shadows.

"Yes?" he asked, setting down the notebook.

Nadir stepped into the light donning a pillow over her midsection. "Hello, Doctor," she said. A muffled burst-shot exploded behind the pillow, slapping Dr. Mengele right against the wall. Blood streaked freely from three fresh bullet holes in his left arm.

"You- You shot me!" he cried. He was too busy looking down to scrutinize the details of his assailant.

"Shh. Not too loud, or the next one is through the head," Nadir warned.

Dr. Mengele looked stunned when he registered her voice. He gasped, "You?! How did you escape?!"

"We're a lot smarter than you ever gave us credit. Remember that little game we played down in the cell? Well, I quite liked it. I thought we could play again."

Nadir threw Dr. Mengele a noose she'd fashioned from bedsheets in an empty infirmary across the hall. "Put that around your neck," she instructed.

"I will not be subjected to this! How dare you-"

Nadir shot him again in the same arm. She practically blew the pillow in half trying to silence it. "Nobody's coming to save you. It's just you and me. Put the fucking thing around your neck, or I'll blast your arm clean off the socket."

Dr. Mengele reluctantly slid the noose over his neck with his uninjured arm. "Now what?" he beckoned.

Nadir dropped the shredded pillow and grabbed the bedsheet. She tossed it over a ceiling beam and pulled it tight, forcing Dr. Mengele to stand upright. He grabbed hold with his uninjured arm until Nadir waved the gun and warned, "Ah-ah." She pulled the sheet until Dr. Mengele stood on his tiptoes then tied the loose end to the door handle.

The tight noose rendered speaking a chore. "If you think I'll t-talk-" he managed to say.

Nadir's rage flooded to the surface. Her cold hard expression perturbed even Dr. Mengele. "Even if you did talk, I wouldn't believe you. You're a snake in human form. There's only one way to deal with the likes of you." She stepped over to a cabinet and began rummaging.

"What are you doing?" he struggled to say.

"You gave a lesson to your cadets the other day. However, you failed to notice you had an extra student present- Me."

She returned with a syringe and a bottle of Sodium Pentothal.

"No! Stop!"

She filled the syringe and then walked over to Dr. Mengele. "Thanks for educating me. I really don't have time to shoot you up with everything." She stuck the needle right into his neck and injected.

"That stuff worked immediately for me. Scream again, and I swear to God you're dead," she said, shoving the MP-40 barrel against his chest. "Are you having fun yet?" she asked.

"Not the least fucking bit," he scowled.

"Good. The stuff seems to be working." She gave him a little slack to allow him better speaking. "Let's test it out. Doctor, why do you hate Jews?"

"The *Führer* hates Jews. Me? I could give a shit. I saw an opportunity to explore my darkest fantasies, and I went for it." He looked shocked by his own words. Perhaps he'd never even contemplated it himself.

Nadir dragged a chair next to Dr. Mengele and commanded, "Step up." Only when she raised the submachine gun did he comply.

She walked over to the door handle and adjusted the bedsheet for the extra slack. She didn't care to know what else lurked in the doctor's pervasive mind.

"Did I positively ID Klaus Barbie and Hermann Michael in the forest?" she asked.

"Yes."

"Are there more from the S.S. High command hiding here?"

"Yes?"

"Many more?"

"Yes!"

"You're raising and training kids here. You're also calling more of your kin to this place. What exactly are you planning?"

"This is the nest where we'll hatch the Fourth Reich."

Nadir cocked her head doubtfully. "You can't possibly hope to achieve that. Even if we hadn't found this place, it couldn't have lasted for much longer. Eventually, you'd have been caught. And then what? You won't ever have armies like the Third Reich did."

"Nor will we need them," he affirmed. "You won't escape. We're looking for your friends as we speak, and Von Schwangau is on the hunt. He knows these trees better than the Black Forest. You can bet your friends are dead, Jewess."

Nadir scoffed. "My team can handle themselves. As for this place, how do you believe a few hundred can retake the world?"

"Nuclear weapons," he said.

Nadir felt the air leave her lungs. The truth and matter-of-fact manner in which he said it caused her to take a half step back. "But... But you don't have a nuclear bomb?"

Dr. Mengele averted his eyes. The move served as an answer within itself. Nadir's face warped with horror. "You're telling me you people have an A-bomb?!"

"Yes," Dr. Mengele leaked.

"Here?!"

"Yes."

"What are you doing with it?"

"We're going to wipe Manhattan off the face of the earth."

"You want revenge against the United States that badly?"

"Hardly. The attack will signal a global call to arms against America. Russia will be at your doorstep within an hour of its detonation. And after you dogs tear each other to shreds, only then will we emerge as the true masters."

"Where is the bomb?" Nadir asked.

"Loaded aboard the U-boat by the lake."

It was too much information for Nadir to remain still. "Doctor, I have one final question..." she began. The question seemed almost too ridiculous even to ask. But then she remembered where she was and everything that had transpired. If all these figures could escape here, then maybe...

"What about Hitler? Is he here?" she blurted.

"Yes, the *Führer* is alive," Dr. Mengele leaked. She could tell he struggled with all his might to fight off the concoction.

Nadir felt her jaw gaping. "Where?"

"Heavily guarded in the center of the compound."

"And Eva Braun? Is she here too?"

"No, she's dead."

"What happened?"

"We needed a body for the Allies to find. She and the *Führer* made a pact, but for good reason, the *Führer* had better intentions. He tricked her into pulling the trigger first."

The sound of nearby gunfire interrupted their intimacy. Nadir blasted Dr. Mengele's uninjured arm and kicked the chair away.

Dr. Mengele flailed and squirmed, legs kicking like a ballet dancer as he gasped for his last breaths. She excused herself before he could asphyxiate. She wasn't like him. Evil or not, she took no pleasure in watching others die.

CHAPTER 33

THE RISING MOON sent little white fingers peeking through the trees.
The loud jungle served as white noise to mask most of their footsteps.
Still, they walked like they were on eggshells. Thompson halted
everyone when a bush rustled a few meters in front of them. They
raised their MP-40s in unison.

The noise ceased. A nervous bead of sweat rolled off Thompson's
forehead and dropped to his combat boot. The bushes stirred at
the sound.

Thompson signaled for an approach. Everyone's fingers wrapped
delicately around their triggers. Thompson extended a tense hand to
peel back the bushes.

A capybara sat on the other side of the bush, scratching its head.
It looked right at them, stood up, and leisurely walked away.

Thompson exhaled. He let the bush snap back and motioned to
move on.

They stripped the dead Nazis bare in the high grass. Nobody
liked the idea of wearing hunting cloaks bearing swastikas, but it
afforded invaluable confusion against the enemy.

An expansive hill with near-vertical inclines took two hours to
scale in the dark. Once they were all the way up top, they stopped to

observe their surroundings. "Bar, can you scale this tree and tell us what you see?" Thompson asked.

"Let me take a look," Bar-Yochai said. He climbed a Wimba tree all the way to the top branch. He stood on the highest branch looking down over the valley. Moonlight brightly colored the land. He could see the Amazon river divided the U-shaped valley in half. Ahead, the moon glimmered against a massive lake. He took out a spy scope for a better glimpse, trailing along the lakeshore.

He stopped when he noticed a lone torch burning beneath an unusual shadow eclipsing a portion of the shoreline. He realized the shadow belonged to a large veil blanketing the entire encampment. "Son of a bitch," he whispered. He climbed down and wiped off his hands. He said no words, just nodded.

"You actually saw it?" Vadim doubted.

"I think so. Maybe three clicks from here, the river spills into a big lake," he pointed. "I saw a torch burning near the shore. I counted at least a dozen buildings hidden under some sort of tarp. No doubt, that's the village."

All hands looked to Thompson for guidance. "We have enough firepower to hold our own, at least for a while," he said. "We'll creep maybe two hundred yards from the place and split up. Vadim and I will create a distraction to draw out whoever's in the village. While they come after us, Bar and Herschel, you guys will infiltrate, grab Nadir, and get out. Once you have her, each group makes for the extraction point on their own."

"Got it," Herschel said. Vadim and Bar-Yochai nodded.

"Vadim, I know you don't like it, but we absolutely need those amphetamines now. Let's dose up just a little more and hydrate. I want to be stalking those krauts before midnight hits."

Vadim resigned himself and divvied up another Pervitin tablet.

CHAPTER 34

VON SCHWANGAU GLIDED through the high grass like a shark cutting waves. Rain or shine, foliage or clearing, it made no difference. The jungle belonged to him, and despite countless dangers, he strived to remain at the top of the food chain. The sea used to be his, and when the Allies stole it, he took to his new environment with apex ambition. He was a beast on the hunt, and killer instinct told him his prey was drawing near.

He stopped at the scent of death hovering in a clearing. Only a few flies had gathered, but their significance was unmistakable. It was precisely the slaughter he'd predicted. The Jews hadn't even bothered to hide the dead. He noted four were stripped of their hunting cloaks. Several were missing guns, and not a single one had any ammunition to speak of.

The hunt intensifies, Von Schwangau thought to himself. *And Eichmann and Mengele will have to answer for the dead.*

He ran a few hundred meters beyond the clearing, stopping again when his ears detected something.

German voices signified it wasn't his targets. He grimaced at the *Hitlerjugend's* poor exhibition of stealth. The distinct voice of Dieter stood out amongst the group. He would have to inform Eichmann to scold the boy later.

Unbeknownst to the *Hitlerjugend* squad, Von Schwangau trailed just a few feet behind them. He loved following strangers through town as a youth. He'd select them at random, taking notes and learning all he could throughout an afternoon. At sea, he'd stalk ships for hours before attacking, savoring the moment like a drink. He liked to do the same with the cadets. The youths revealed quite a lot when they thought it was just them and the trees.

He crept close enough to eavesdrop. It wasn't their incessant school gossip that fascinated him so. It was the way they carried themselves. He remembered being their age. *How strange it must be, living so far from their natural home,* he thought. All the sweeter it would be when he rectified their birthrights.

He became so preoccupied in his heroic fantasy, he didn't realize how close he'd gotten. At arm's reach, he withdrew into the shadows. The youths had no idea he was ever even there.

The hour grew late, but even into nightfall, Von Schwangau stayed on the hunt. He could feel his crossbow, *Heimi*, thirsting for blood. He always named his weapons, this one for the Germanic hero of ancient times. The old crossbow was a ransacked treasure from a history museum in Munich. They could sell it for a fortune, but the money was better spent keeping it in his deadly hands.

After forging the iron mask, the skilled village metallurgist fashioned the finest arrow bolts Von Schwangau had ever seen. He had one loaded and ready to fire at a moment's notice.

Over the hills, he climbed, and then down the other side into the thick-forested valley. A patch of moonlight illuminated boot prints in the mud that weren't his own. He knelt at one of the prints and tilted his mask back to sample the soil against his lips. It hadn't rained for hours. The mud's fickle texture clued Von Schwangau the print was less than an hour old. To his prey's credit, they were covering a great deal of ground in remarkable time. He wondered if they knew they were drawing so close to the village. No doubt, they hadn't a clue he was close behind.

The squawking bird species signified the hour neared midnight. Quiet as a phantom, Von Schwangau prowled through the trees, ears primed like his crossbow.

Then he heard them. Faintly. No more than a hundred yards ahead, at most.

He inched closer. The Jews spoke in muffled English, a tongue he despised yet passably understood. He hadn't heard the dialect in many years, and it took his ears a moment to comprehend. He moved even closer.

"We'll count to one hundred and begin the assault. You guys check every last building if you have to. Even if it leads underground."

"What if we can't find her?"

"Vadim and I will hold them off as long as we can. I'm counting on you guys to tear that place apart."

Von Schwangau hovered just a few feet behind the one who shot at him earlier. He contemplated his move carefully. He'd fire an arrow bolt point-blank, drop the crossbow, and then shoot the rest dead with his Mauser.

Just as Von Schwangau raised the crossbow to his shoulder, his shifting weight cracked a branch. The Jews turned around and looked right at him.

Von Schwangau's snapped back the trigger, but the one who shot at him ducked out of the way just in time. The arrow bolt stabbed into a tree instead.

Automatic gunfire erupted right in Von Schwangau's face. He ducked behind a tree just as bullets showered.

"Go!" he heard one cry.

Their footsteps split up. He slung the crossbow around his back and donned the Mauser.

The gunshots stirred the nearby *Hitlerjugend*. He could hear them closing in. "Over here!" he shouted.

Gunfire spat back, slicing through branches and leaves. Von Schwangau stole a glance around the tree to see a muzzle flashing some thirty feet off.

He waited for a pause in the action, then leaped from his hiding spot to dash in an arch toward the muzzle flash.

The gun fired wildly in the same direction without adjusting. The Jews certainly didn't count on him hearing their plan. He knew what they were doing.

Von Schwangau slithered up from the side, Mauser poised and ready. The MP-40 spat controlled bursts, over and over without any real cognition behind the shots.

He neared the firing weapon, raised his Mauser, and emptied it shooting. But after his magazine emptied, the MP-40 still kept firing. Then it stopped. Von Schwangau got right up to the gun and felt terror erupt inside him.

Somehow the Jews had rigged two different MP-40s to a branch with strings attached to the triggers. He'd foolishly walked right into their trap.

Every muscle in his body suddenly wanted to retreat, yet soldierly expertise told him it already was too late. Just as he turned around, his veteran instinct proved accurate. He faced the business end of a Colt 1911.

From the moment he set foot in Brazil, he knew he was on borrowed time. He should have died years ago, condemned to a watery grave like the rest of the wolf *Kapitäns*. He didn't even have time to manifest a final thought. The gun fired right in his face.

CHAPTER 35

VADIM KNEELED over Von Schwangau to check his pulse. "Save the bullet. He's dead, Thompson."

Thompson aimed at Von Schwangau's unarmored chest and said, "I hit the mask."

"You shot him point blank with a .45. His brains are probably oozing out through his ears. Let's keep moving," Vadim suggested.

Thompson hesitantly tucked his 1911 away. He kicked Von Schwangau once in the chest and growled, "Let's hear that Nazi song now."

Germanic voices called out from both sides. Thompson fired a quick MP-40 volley in each direction as bullets peppered the vicinity. Dirt and leaves exploded everywhere. Thompson and Vadim fell low to the ground covering their heads. "You take three o'clock, I'll take nine," Thompson said.

"Roger," Vadim said.

The shooting ceased. The two stood shoulder-to-shoulder returning fire in opposite directions. Echoing screams confirmed they each hit something.

"Move!" Thompson barked. They only ran a dozen paces before German lead forced them flat against the ground.

They crawled to a tree and traded spent MP magazines for fresh replacements. "So, are we keeping score?" Vadim asked coyly.

"Stay alive- we all win," Thompson affirmed. "Ready?"

Vadim nodded.

They sprang to their feet, raising their MPs and spraying the area ahead. They shed their spent magazines and slapped in reloads as they took cover behind another thick tree.

"Love these things," Vadim said, examining his MP-40.

"Speak for yourself," Thompson replied. "Wish I had a Tommy gun about now."

Voices screaming frantic German were only a stone's throw away. Thompson peered around the tree to see dozens of muzzle flashes. Behind them, countless torches sprang to life from the village.

"It's working," Thompson said.

Vadim peeked around the tree. "Haven't been in a fight like this for-"

Bark exploded right above their heads. Muzzle flashes suddenly flanked them from all sides. They had to abandon the tree and army-crawl away.

The gunfire paused a minute later. "They're not here!" a German voice cried.

"Spread out!" shouted another.

Thompson and Vadim froze. A lone Nazi girl stepped just three feet in front of them. Her eyes danced right over their camouflaged cloaks. Vadim motioned to attack. Thompson shook his head. The girl moved on.

But not far enough. Vadim cracked a branch as he attempted to stand. The girl turned back and brought her MP-40 to shoulder-level.

Thompson and Vadim dove away firing at her. She went down in a moonlit blood mist. They didn't have time to check the kill. More Nazis were charging.

Vadim raised his MP-40 to fire, but Thompson directed the barrel down with his hand. "Let them get closer," he said.

Heinrich, the nineteen-year-old *Hitlerjugend* squad leader, had seen combat as young as ten fighting bravely against the Russians. He hadn't seen action since the fall of Berlin, and this time, his home would not be taken.

"Open fire!" he shouted. His squad unleashed hellfire into the trees. They blew through their magazines, replenished, and spent those too.

"I think we got 'em," Heinrich said, changing out a fresh magazine. "Let's hit them with another just in case."

Thompson and Vadim sprung up and unleashed an end-to-end spray. They ravaged the entire squad within half a second.

It bought just a moment's reprieve. Nazi gunfire raked first from the left, then more joining in from the right.

Every Nazi they killed, Thompson and Vadim stole a fresh MP or a magazine. Each had enough guns decorated on their ensemble to be considered articles of clothing. But crawling with so many firearms proved challenging. They huddled together at the base of a redwood tree. They were so close to the village their bullets could hit the buildings.

"Back-to-back in a three-sixty burst, 'til each of us runs empty," Thompson said.

"Roger," Vadim replied.

"Now!" Thompson yelled. Together they stood back-to-back, rotating and firing in a complete circle. The instant their bullets stopped, shots erupted again from all sides. They fell to the ground covering their heads.

"They're boxing us in," Vadim said as he slapped in a new magazine. He aimed from the ground and fired. The MP clicked when he pulled the trigger. He tossed the gun aside and tried another MP off his ensemble, only to have that one click, too.

"Told you," Thompson said. "You know what doesn't jam?"

"Yeah, yeah," Vadim scowled. He got a burst shot off on his third MP. He blew through the magazine shooting from the ground and then ejected it. "We're burning through six magazines a minute, T. This can't go on forever," he said as he inserted another.

Adrenaline and amphetamines clouded Thompson's thoughts. He felt so hopped up, he started believing he could rush and kill them all with his bare hands. Then a bullet zinged by and scraped his arm. He suddenly remembered he was profoundly impaired. "Don't fire a shot," he said. "Just keep up." He sprang to his feet and broke into a mad dash.

"Goddammit," Vadim muttered. He jumped up and dashed after Thompson.

They raced through the trees. Bullets skipped by all around them, but thick jungle cover and their lightning agility kept them free of injury.

They dashed right into a group of adult Nazis. Some of the militia had served in combat, but most- like *Oberführer* Walter Weber- were former Nazi aristocrats. They had little training and even less courage. Seeing Thompson and Vadim, clad in *Hitlerjugend* garb, they didn't know how to react. The confusion cost them all their lives.

Thompson and Vadim briefly searched the dead. "MP. MP. MP. It's all they've got here," Thompson complained.

Gunfire howled from the other end of the village. "Herschel and Bar-Yochai must be getting busy," Vadim commented.

The nighttime jungle sounds were briefly quelled when a Germanic voice boomed over a loudspeaker: "All hands, return to base! The intruders are attacking!"

"Sounds like the jig is up," Vadim said.

"Time to advance," Thompson said.

The tree line to the first building in the village offered a hundred yards of open space. They had no choice but to make a break for it. Vadim issued cover fire from the rear as Thompson ran. He reached the building and secured additional cover fire until Vadim was at his side.

Nazi militiamen engaged from the other side of the building.

Vadim traded burst shots around the corner while Thompson turned his MP against the wood and squeezed the trigger. The structure absorbed every bullet.

"Those nine millimeters will never penetrate," Vadim said.

Bullets impacted the wood to Vadim's right. He and Thompson glanced up to see a torch-wielding Nazi firing a Walther at them. The two raised their MPs and gunned him down with ease.

"I've got an idea. Cover me," Thompson said. He bolted away from the building to grab the torch and then raced back.

Vadim bore an evil grin when Thompson returned. "Oh, Thompson, you're not going to-"

Thompson blasted out a window and flung the torch inside. The building's dry-wood interior went up in blazes so fast, they had to stand back.

The Nazis on the other side fled as flames licked high to spark the tentpoles first, then to catch the camouflaged netting above. Its water-repellant nylon material combusted like gunpowder to light the whole sky red.

"This whole Nazi nest is about to go up like a campfire," Vadim grinned with a face colored orange.

Showering fire lit the way as Thompson and Vadim combed the village back-to-back. Everything the raining molten nets touched immediately went up in flames.

"We'll call this the second fall of Berlin," Vadim laughed.

A tall, stocky Nazi charged around the corner bearing an StG-44 assault rifle. Vadim saw him just in the nick of time to fire. His MP-40 clicked.

The Nazi speckled just a few shots off. Vadim drew his .38 snub nose and blasted him away. Thompson missed a bullet by mere inches.

Vadim kicked the dead Nazi over and said, "I'll be damned, Thompson. Look who I just plugged!"

Thompson raised his gun to fire on a Nazi lurking in Vadim's shadow. The bullets tore equally close past his head before slamming into the Nazi's throat.

"We'll call it even," Vadim said unamused.

"I told you- No scores. Who'd you shoot?"

The first man down had a single bullet wound to his forehead. His dead eyes stared blankly at the heavens, face illuminated by the raging fires all around.

"That's Hermann Michel," Vadim said. He swung his backpack off his shoulder and opened it up.

"What are you doing?" Thompson asked.

"Snapping a photo for Fink," he said, quickly assembling his camera.

"Vadim, we got him. Let's move."

Vadim ignored him.

"Vadim!" Thompson yelled, tackling him down. He gunned down a Nazi trio charging right at them.

"Thanks," Vadim mumbled. He snapped a quick photo of Hermann.

"No more," Thompson said. He threw off his last MP-40 and peeled Hermann's StG out of his cold dead hands. "That's more like it," he said, checking the gun. He'd always hated German guns, especially the MP-40. At least the *Sturmgewehr-44* was a proper rifle.

A bullet hit Vadim's camera right out of his hand and blew it into a million pieces. Eight more sliced past him, but the only thing on his mind was preserving the film. He dove and caught the spool before it could hit the damp dirt.

Thompson spit back bullets with his mighty StG. The Nazis were instantly ravaged. "Now let's get the hell out of here," Thompson said. "Back to back again."

Most of the buildings were burning now. Come the following day, the crows would feast. Bodies and bullet casings littered the place everywhere Thompson and Vadim looked. "Looks like Bar and Hersch really went to town," Thompson said.

"Pun intended," Vadim hooted.

Thunder rumbled from above. Lightning flashes minimalized the blazing fires.

"Blood and honor!" a voice screamed in German.

They whirled around to double-face the threat: A lone teenage boy cradling a Walther MKb. Four youths fell in on either side, all equipped with StGs. Then six more Nazi militiamen joined behind with MP-40s.

"Shit," Thompson said.

They took a few faltering steps back, raised their guns, and fired as they fled. The Nazis unleashed a wave of bullets obliterating the buildings behind them.

Thompson and Vadim ducked through a gap between two buildings. "Draw them back to the trees!" Thompson shouted.

Rain broke from the skies like a dam. Water poured onto the village and quelled the fires with an ominous loud hiss.

Bleeding bodies of all the fallen Nazis turned the muddy village streets red.

They tore around a blind corner and came face to face with another lone youth. In his tiny arms, he held an MG-30 machine gun. It was so heavy he couldn't even bring it up to aim.

"Drop it!" Thompson barked in German. If the kid brought it any higher, Thompson had to fire. "Please! Just run and hide!"

Tears streaked down the boy's face. His arms shook with uncertainty. "I'm sorry!" he squeaked. He dropped the gun in the mud and fled.

"Here," Thompson said, handing Vadim the StG. He went and picked up the MG-30 for himself. "Kid didn't even load it." He cocked the heavy weapon and brought it to shoulder level. "Let's hope he didn't flood the chamber when he dropped it," he added.

They fell back to the tree line without taking any additional fire. But just before breaching the forest, bullets sailed from the village.

Thompson turned back and squeezed the MG's trigger. Its blinding muzzle flash caused him to squint as the gun spat a monsoon of bullets back at the Nazis. They abandoned all pursuit and dove for cover.

The machine gun's red-hot barrel sizzled against the raindrops. By the time the deafening war machine clicked empty, Thompson's hands ached from the vibration. He dropped the spent weapon in the mud and fell back with Vadim through the trees.

CHAPTER 36

DR. MENGELE WAS A GOOD START, but Nadir still had much to accomplish. She couldn't just turn tail and run, not after all she'd learned, and by the sounds of it, someone else was attacking too. What began as a few distant shots had devolved into an all-out gun battle. She had a good idea who the offending party might be. She'd join them shortly, after she completed the mission.

The U-boat would be her first target. Nobody in the village knew she'd escaped, and she figured they'd be too preoccupied with defense to be guarding the hangar. Hitler, on the other hand, would likely prove challenging.

Her plan came to a violent halt when a fresh bullet hole appeared in the wood inches in front of her nose.

"There! She's wearing our clothes!" a Germanic voice screamed.

Nadir barely had a chance to count them all. Bullets practically disintegrated the very spot she stood as she broke into a retreat. She barreled around a building and then stopped. Uzziel taught her to hold ground in a firefight. She dug her heels in and raised her MP-40 to shoulder level.

Nazis emerged around the corner. She squeezed the trigger as soon as they came into her sights. A few went down while the rest scattered to find cover.

She flipped the MP to semi-auto and fired off a few more burst-rounds until the magazine ran empty. She then retreated through a gap between two buildings, changing out the magazine as she ran.

"Go around and cut her off!" she heard one yell.

She emerged from the gap and collided with a Nazi. She fell against the building, while he fell to the ground. She looked dead into the man's eyes. It was *Klaus Barbie.*

Nadir pointed the MP at his head and smiled.

Barbie couldn't even react. He just incredulously stared up the barrel. "Please," he said. "I'm-"

Nadir unloaded the entire magazine right in his face. By the time the MP ran out, there wasn't much left of his head except a mass of pink and red.

Splintering wood showered her as bullets dotted the vicinity. She slipped through another building gap in retreat. On the other side, a dozen Nazis greeted her. They trained their guns all at once. But their attention briefly shifted upward as a strange red light shined down. "No!" she heard one of them mumble. Fire colored the sky. They directed their full wrath back to her.

She closed her eyes. Evil would prevail, and she would join her family amongst the Nazi's death toll. She pictured Germany before Hitler: *Freedom. Family. Her childhood. Her best memory- a family Shabbat dinner.*

"Fire!" she heard a Nazi yell. But her heart continued beating when the gunfire stopped. She opened her eyes to find all the Nazis dead at her feet. Bar-Yochai and Herschel stood behind them, smoke twirling from the barrels of their MPs.

Nadir fell to her knees praying, "*Baruch atah adonai eloheinu melech ha'olam, hatov vhameitiv.*" She'd stared death in the face so many times that by this point, the two were on a first-name basis.

Bar-Yochai and Herschel both exclaimed her name and embraced her. "We've got you now," Bar-Yochai said. He let go to scan their guard.

Herschel muttered a quick few words in Hebrew, adding, "What a close call. Are you okay?"

"I will be," Nadir said. "What's with all the gunshots?"

"Thompson and Vadim are distracting them. We came for you."

"Did you guys get any intel on this place?" Nadir asked, taking a fresh MP-40 off one of the dead Nazis. She made sure she had a full magazine before cocking the gun.

"Not much. Just that it exists, and they had you captive," Herschel said. "We have to get out of here."

"We can't. Not yet," she said.

"Nadir, there's too many. We have to report this place to Fink."

Nadir shook her head. "No, you guys don't understand. Hitler's not dead. He's here, hiding in one of these buildings. If we run, he might slip away forever."

"Who told you that?" Bar-Yochai said, astonished.

"Doctor Josef Mengele. I shot him full of Sodium Pentothal and hanged him twenty minutes ago. Before he died, he confessed. Hitler's here, and they've also acquired an atom bomb. It's loaded in a U-boat by the lake."

Something stirred behind them. They all pointed their guns.

A mother and her three young children stopped in the middle of the street and threw their hands up.

"Go! Get out of here!" Nadir yelled in German. The mother easily complied.

"No question then. We've got to do something," Herschel said.

Bar-Yochai liberated a few more MPs off the dead Nazis and threw them to his comrades. "Herschel, you take Hitler. Nadir and I will hit the U-boat. Make for the extraction point on your own."

Most of the wooden structures in the village were burning now, but a clap of thunder signified nature was on the way with reprieve. "Any idea which building he's in?" Herschel asked Nadir.

"Somewhere in the village center, I think," Nadir said.

"Shoot to kill," Bar-Yochai said.

"Keep her safe," Herschel replied.

They split up in opposite directions. For the first time since landing in the jungle, Nadir felt safe. Bar-Yochai was a quiet man, and she didn't know him like Uzziel. One thing she did know- he was every bit as deadly, if not more.

Bar-Yochai fired at a Nazi posting up on a rooftop. Nadir hadn't even seen him. The Nazi grunted and dropped like a stone, rolling off the roof and hitting the ground in perfect harmony with a thunderclap.

Rain beat down at a steady pace, sending the fires into a dying hiss. Battle noises from the other side of the village were lulling too. "Thompson and Vadim must be falling back," Bar-Yochai said.

"Are you feeling alright? You seem a bit frazzled," Nadir said.

"Long story. Thompson got us hopped up on speed."

"What?!"

Bar-Yochai smirked. "Desperate times. We did what we had to for you, kid." He fired a burst round down the alley and killed two Nazis waiting to ambush. "Pay attention," he scolded.

He moved Nadir behind him and advanced with silent, catlike steps.

A Nazi woman sprang out behind a building and unloaded on them.

Bar-Yochai traded shots back, and his landed first. The woman went down holding the trigger and sprayed a barrage straight in the air.

A livestock stable cooed with agitation. The nervous animals masked their footsteps as they advanced to the edge of the village. They stopped at a corner building and braced to charge. Bar-Yochai motioned one, two, and then jumped out with Nadir on the count of three.

Lightning lit the way in place of the dying fires. The storm intensified with the battle noises again. "That must be Herschel," Bar Yochai said. Just as Nadir predicted, Nazis failed to guard the hanger.

They pushed open a big wooden door and entered. Their footsteps echoed through the sound of splashing water. Bar-Yochai reached into his backpack and took out a flashlight.

The beam hit the water and scattered light all over the hangar's massive inner expanse. He directed the light upward to focus on a big steel hull. A long swipe of the beam revealed the U-boat suspended in the air by a spider web of chains. Bar-Yochai whistled in amazement.

"Damn thing looks brand new," Nadir said.

"They must have had it fixed up," Bar-Yochai said. He walked the length of the U-boat, stopping midway beneath the craft. "Look at that." He shined the beam on a weld scar just beneath the conning tower.

"What is it?" Nadir asked.

"I bet that's where the bomb is. They couldn't get it in through the tower, and the torpedo tubes are too slim, so they cut it open and stuck it inside." He frowned. "That means it's a suicide mission. To set it off, someone would have to discharge it from within."

"I'm sure they'll have plenty of volunteers."

Bar-Yochai stopped at a rope ladder. He shined the light tracing it all the way up to the top of the conning tower. "Shall we climb inside?"

"Are we stealing it?"

"Don't be ridiculous." He started climbing up the rope ladder. "C'mon," he called.

Nadir followed. "If we can't steal it, what are you planning to do?"

Bar-Yochai ignored the question. They reached the top of the conning tower and climbed inside. Bar-Yochai stuck the flashlight in his mouth to light their descent into the craft.

"Holy hell. It still stinks in here," Nadir said.

Bar-Yochai returned the flashlight to his hand. Minus the smell, the U-boat looked fully-restored.

"I've smelled worse," Bar-Yochai said. He shined the flashlight on the shell of an atomic bomb that just barely fit in the confined space. They could see it had been welded down to the floor.

"It must be Soviet," Nadir said, studying a Russian label taped to the bomb. "Wonder if they know it's even missing?"

"Let's get to work," Bar-Yochai said.

Nadir followed him through U-boat's tight interior to the control panel. She noticed the sounds from outside were muted within the beast's iron belly.

Bar-Yochai shined his light over the control panel. Its intricacy left him scratching his head.

"Should we shoot it?" Nadir asked.

"No. The bullet could ricochet, or worse."

"What, then?"

"We'll blow the engines out," Bar-Yochai said.

"And how do we do that?"

"If we can turn it to full thrust, hanging from chains in the air, it might do the trick."

"Which one of these is the thruster?"

"I don't know," Bar-Yochai said. "Let's see what this does." He pushed a button. Nothing happened. He pushed another. Still, nothing happened.

"This is a worse idea than shooting it," Nadir nagged.

Bar-Yochai pressed another button. Then he pulled a lever. Then pressed another button. This time, battle lights lit the whole cabin red. "Hmm. That did something." He pressed another.

The craft started to hum. "Now we're getting somewhere," he said. He reached for another lever, but instead, Nadir kicked it forward and broke it. The U-boat rattled and lurched in its chains. "C'mon!" Bar-Yochai yelled, grabbing her.

They wobbled out of the shaky U-boat and climbed out. The U-boat's exposed engines ripping at full power was deafening. They tried to shield their ears as they scaled down the rope ladder. Once on the ground, Bar-Yochai shouted, "Run for it!"

The U-boat rocked from its chains. Once the first link snapped, it was all over. The link ricocheted a dozen times around the hangar and then struck a second link. From there, the entire chain-web snapped apart. The U-boat plunged into the water and shot forward at full thrust, ripping part of the hangar down with it.

Bar-Yochai and Nadir watched in amazement as the unmanned U-boat jetted into the lake dragging massive fragments of wood from its chains. The leviathan tilted sideways to expose the open conning tower to the water. The U-boat sunk without so much as a spark.

CHAPTER 37

"No more," Vadim warned Thompson. "Your heart can't take it."

"Just one more piece," Thompson begged.

"Goddammit. If you have a heart attack, I'll have enough Jewish guilt left over to fill my next five lives." Vadim reluctantly broke a Pervitin tablet into pieces and handed Thompson a small fragment. "That's it," he said.

There hadn't been a shot fired in hours. Moments after fleeing into the forest, a terrible sound crashed from the lake and drew all the Nazis away. Thompson and Vadim easily lost the token few who pursued them. Neither had an inkling how much ground they'd covered since.

Thompson's ears continued to ring from battle. Only when Vadim nudged him did he realize he couldn't hear anything. "What?" he asked.

"I said what do you think the commotion was that drew them away?"

"No idea," Thompson responded.

The edged through the daunting jungle night, stopping briefly at daybreak. Thompson licked his chapped lips. His head pounded from amphetamine withdrawal, and his mouth felt dry as a bone.

"Let's slow the pace down," Vadim suggested. "We've been awake nearly two days now. Whatever tail we had, they're long gone."

Thompson recognized exhaustion once they stopped moving. It was the first bit of rest his body had enjoyed for twelve hours. He suddenly realized every muscle below his hips radiated pain. He noticed he had to pee, too. He went and relieved himself against a tree. Vadim tossed him his water canteen once he finished and watched as Thompson gulped the entire bottle.

"You should eat a ration bar," Vadim said.

"Not hungry."

"Don't make me mother bird you. Your body desperately needs the calories. Please, I'm not asking."

Thompson reached into his sack, took out a ration bar, peeled back the wrapper, and shoved the whole thing into his mouth. He grimaced as he forced it down, only to dry-heave. "Water," he gagged.

Vadim took out his reserve canteen and handed it over. "You good?"

"You might be right. We'll slow it down," Thompson admitted.

Snapping twigs seized their attention. All they had left for ammo was in their handguns. They held their breath and got low to the ground as they silently took out their sidearms. Thompson signaled he would take the lead. Vadim nodded obediently.

They sprung out. A hulking figure with a slim companion stopped dead in their tracks and slowly turned around. It was Bar-Yochai and Nadir.

Thompson and Vadim immediately tucked their guns away and rushed to embrace Nadir. "I'm so glad you're safe!" Thompson gushed.

"Where's Herschel?" Vadim asked.

They shook their heads unknowingly. "We split up," Bar-Yochai said. "Nadir and I went after one target, he went after another."

"Target?" Thompson questioned. "What target?"

Bar-Yochai smirked. "Nadir has quite a story."

Her words left Thompson and Vadim speechless. "So that loud crash was the U-boat sinking. And the other shots were Herschel..."

Dawn came upon them. They moved at a much slower pace now. All Bar-Yochai could think about was sleep. Thompson wasn't much better, though the additional Pervitin fragment gave him a second wind. At the top of a hill, a gap in the trees allowed a glimpse of the valley. They could see smoke wisps rising high in the sky a few kilometers behind them.

"Rain or shine, that place is going to smoke for quite a while after last night," Thompson said. "Whether or not Herschel had any luck, we'll just have to wait and see."

The faint engine of a plane could be heard flying low over the trees.

"That's a single-engine fighter if I've ever heard one," Bar-Yochai said.

"Here it comes," Vadim said.

They rushed out of sight and ducked down. The plane shot by overhead and disappeared over the hill.

"We're clear," Thompson said.

"That looked like a British fighter. How do you suppose they got it?" Vadim said.

"That's the least of our concerns. It's coming back," Thompson announced.

Everyone ducked and covered as the plane thundered by again. It flew so low that it even kicked up dirt.

Thompson squinted through the trees to track the plane as it circled the valley like a falcon searching for prey.

"That's going to kill progress if we have to keep hiding," Bar-Yochai said.

"He won't fly after dark. Plus, he doesn't know we're down here. He'd have shot if he did," Thompson said.

Vadim scowled. "Let's just hope he hits a flock of birds."

The plane circled the valley for hours. Every time it passed overhead, everyone hid. It flew low enough to hit with a stone, but the thick foliage kept them concealed.

Finally, after a whole day of hiding, the plane flew one final lap and then turned back for the village. They gained significant ground despite the challenge it posed. Smoke from the village was now too distant to see.

Thompson beckoned a break at twilight. The Pervitin had worn off, and again, his body battled exhaustion. His comrades fared no better. They only had three ration bars left amongst the group. Thompson still didn't have an appetite. Vadim forced him to eat a bar regardless. He nearly blew a blood vessel in his eye from dry-heaving afterward. "We ready to move?" he squeaked after a twenty-minute recovery period.

"Only if you are," Vadim said.

The submersible was due at dawn, and it would be a long hike through the night to reach it. Central Intelligence would wait as long as they could, but the question lingered in Thompson's mind about what to do if Herschel failed to appear.

"Shut the fuck up," he thought he heard Herschel say.

Surely, he wasn't having auditory hallucinations?

"Did you guys hear that?" Nadir whispered.

They all heard a thump and an ensuing grunt. They crept around a tree and peeked.

Herschel was too preoccupied beating the living shit out of a man tied up with a pillowcase covering his head.

"Piece-of-fucking-human-waste-you-dirty-rotten-"

"Herschel?" Thompson asked.

Herschel turned around. Sweat ran freely off his forehead. His commandeered Nazi cloak was tattered and caked in mud and blood. Undoubtedly it was that of his foes. "Oh, hey fellas. Just in time!" he smiled. He scraped his prisoner off the ground, yanked off the pillowcase, and tossed him before the group. "I couldn't carry him anymore, so I was about to beat him to death," he gleamed. "Does anyone have a better idea?"

His mustache was shaved and his hair unkempt, but his face was unmistakable. There in the mud sat Adolf Hitler.

CHAPTER 38

HERSCHEL GINSBERG WAS A BORN FIGHTER. As a teen in the mean streets of South Boston, he nearly got killed standing up for a friend against a gang of five boys. He took the first two with ease. But then he got cocky. One of the boys snuck up with a metal trash can and bashed him over the back of the head. He spent three weeks in the hospital, and he gladly would have done it again. It was his sense of conviction. It took the form of loyalty as a youth, and patriotism as a grown man. Together, these fires forged a soldier known by his wartime colleagues as "The Hammer." Fearless and bold, everyone who served with The Hammer knew him to be a champion dancer in the ballrooms of combat and death. He was a mighty storm that hadn't been seen by the likes of Hitler's henchmen for years... Until tonight.

Every step Herschel took, empty shell casings filled his boot-prints. He wielded an MP-40 in each hand as he marched through the village lighting the way with gunfire. His trigger-fingers shredded anything that moved.

Burst-fire shots colored the faces of twelve advancing Nazis. Their bullets whistled right past Herschel's head. He fired both MPs until their magazines ran empty, cast them aside, and dive-rolled.

Seven were dead by the time he dove. He emerged from the roll firing his 1911. The American-made lead caught the first Nazi in the lower jaw. It tore and crushed at the same time as it ripped through his throat and out the back of his neck. He lethally tapped the rest with single head-shots. All the Nazis slumped dead against a building, brains oozing down the wood and dripping onto their lifeless bodies.

Herschel liberated two fresh MPs from their corpses. There wasn't much of his face left to identify, but Herschel swore one of the bodies was that of Adolf Eichmann.

Right as he turned around, retaliating gunshots erupted all around him. He fell to the ground firing, his shots more of a scattered shower to cover his escape.

Those who avoided injury sought cover behind a building. The rest bled out shamelessly in the dirt.

The battle briefly quelled when the nets above erupted in flames. A scrap of burning net landed right on Herschel's shoulder. He patted it out muttering Hebrew.

"Good lord," he said, looking around. Most of the buildings were up in embers. Rebuilding would be an impossible task if there were any survivors at all.

Herschel kept firing as he fell back around a burning building. He peeked around the corner and counted ten Nazis. He jumped out, but his guns ran empty after just a moment of full-auto.

Reprisal Nazi gunfire forced Herschel back. He threw aside the spent MPs and donned his 1911 again. He circled around the building and snuck up behind the Germans.

Eight shots rang out. The Nazis didn't even have time to turn before The Hammer nailed them all dead.

Smoke coiled from his 1911. He paused to listen. The other firefight grew quiet, signifying Thompson and Vadim were falling back. That meant Herschel's timetable was ticking away.

He kicked over a few of the fallen dead and smiled upon finding an StG-44. "Bingo," he said. He kneeled and unburdened the cadaver of its rifle and ammunition.

Herschel found six Nazis guarding a lone building in front of the temple. Four held StGs, while the other two stood over a mounted MG-42 machine gun.

The allies nicknamed the MG-42 "Hitler's Buzzsaw," and Herschel was all too familiar with its menacing capabilities. His brain registered it just as the Nazis opened fire. He dove in the nick of time, mud flying up all around him. The 7.92x55 millimeter rounds chewed through the wood and rained splinters everywhere. He kept his head down and waited for them to change out the barrel when the gun got too hot.

The Nazis fired at least five hundred rounds on Herschel before their onslaught came to an unnerving close. Then a great crash boomed from the direction of the lake, sidelining their attention.

Herschel seized the distraction to pop out and unleash hell. He changed out his magazine as he stepped over the dead and approached the building. He tried to open it, but the door was locked. He blasted the handle off and kicked the door in.

Inside was dark and vacant. In the far corner, torchlight emitted from a spacious hole in the ground. He approached with his rifle trained.

The spider hole had a ladder, but Herschel couldn't afford to be careless. He peered down into the hole. It was only an eight-foot drop. He bent his knees a few times for practice, poised his gun, and then dropped into the hole.

Herschel's feet hit the ground in conjunction with the squeeze of his trigger. The StG firing in such a confined space was both deafening and awesomely powerful. The two Nazi guards were blown away in an explosive blood mist. Even all the candles shuddered.

"Don't move!" Herschel screamed in German.

There was a bed in the very back of the spider hole. An unarmed Nazi attendant standing next to the bed had his hands raised up. A petrified-looking Hitler sat in the bed.

"Please, don't shoot," the attendant squeaked. Herschel answered his plea with two shots to the chest. Again, the candles shuddered. Hitler cowered like a fawn.

"Get up," Herschel barked.

Hitler murmured a merciful Germanic plea. Herschel screamed, "Now!" He shoved the gun barrel against Hitler's cheek and sizzled the flesh upon contact. Hitler yelped and raised from the bed with his trembling, Parkinsons-ridden hands as high as they could reach.

Herschel longed to shoot the old dictator right then and there, but it wouldn't be fair to his comrades. His task was to find the man, not to issue justice.

He smacked Hitler in the back of the head with the butt-end of his rifle and then set to work binding his hands with torn bedsheets. He slipped off a pillowcase and stuck it over Hitler's head, then hoisted him over his shoulder. He was light and frail, and despite being unconscious, his body still tremored violently.

Herschel strung the machine gun over his other shoulder and climbed out of the spider hole. He shifted Hitler to wrap him like a scarf over his neck so that he could wield the StG using both hands.

Outside in the rain, a few Nazis were waiting for him outside. He gunned down two with ease. The rest scurried for cover behind a sizzling building.

Herschel dropped Hitler in the mud and commandeered the MG-42 off its mount. He quickly loaded a fresh barrel, fed it a new ammunition belt, and indiscriminately opened fire. He shot until it overheated and then cast it aside like trash. He scooped Hitler out of the mud and stole away into the jungle.

They wandered for hours. Every time Hitler awoke, Herschel beat him over the head. He couldn't make Hitler walk. He was too feeble, and if he were to die, it certainly wouldn't be at nature's hands. Not if Herschel could help it.

After nearly a day, Herschel was exhausted. The Pervitin had worn off, and by this point, the taxing jungle odyssey depleted all that remained of his strength. So, when Hitler awoke for the tenth time just before sunset, Herschel decided he'd had enough. He threw the old man off his shoulders and began beating him unmercifully. It was something straight out of every enlisted man's fantasy who fought in Europe. Somehow it didn't feel nearly as satisfying as it should have.

Herschel started swearing as he dialed up the beating. Even still, it was a dish that tasted lacking... until his friends arrived. Their company proved precisely the missing ingredient.

The looks on their faces when Herschel pulled the pillowcase off Hitler's head was worth every ounce of agony they'd endured since deploying to the jungle. There Nesher Unit stood, united with the ultimate prize before them and nobody to intervene except Adonai himself. Something told them God was looking the other way.

"What should we do with him?" Vadim asked. Everyone stared Hitler with deep sickening disdain.

Thompson squatted down to Hitler's level and peered into his eyes. Perhaps it was the heat, but he swore he could hear the screams of all his victims coming from those deep blue pits. "Are you ready to face justice?" Thompson asked him in German.

Hitler sucked back a mouthful of air and spat right in Thompson's face. He merely wiped it off and grinned. "And here I thought I wouldn't get a proper shower until I was home."

"Nadir," Thompson said, "I'll let you do the honors. Tell him who we are, what we've done, and what's going to happen to the rest of his people."

Nadir nodded and began explaining the situation in German. Thompson stared hard, smiling as Hitler's arrogant scowl cracked and then fully crumbled.

"I still win," Hitler griped when Nadir was done.

They all looked mystified to each other. "How do you figure?" Thompson asked.

Hitler scoffed. "Bring me to justice?! Unveiling me back to the world will only serve to inspire. We may have gone underground, we may have been temporarily defeated, but rest assured, the likes of you will never stomp out our cause."

Thompson smirked. "We're not like you, Adolf. Not in the least bit. We're not monsters obsessed with racial purity. We are champions of justice and ensuring none of your comrades escape it is our sworn duty. Before we came here, we took down twenty-two of your men. Those we captured, we offered a fair trial, but everyone chose death instead. You, on the other hand, will receive no such choice in the matter. The fact you've made it this far is a shattering blow to the name of justice."

Thompson paused. "You're right. The truth would be toxic. The Third Reich ended in 1945. You never escaped Berlin, and the body we leave here in these woods will be food for flies, and nothing more."

He turned to Vadim and said, "Give me the medical pack."

Vadim unzipped his bag and took out the pack. Thompson extracted a leather booklet and opened it to show Hitler a syringe. "Hold him down and keep him quiet. They might still be out there," Thompson commanded.

Bar-Yochai and Herschel each took Hitler by the arm and pinned him to the dirt. Vadim and Nadir got his legs. Hitler's protests were muted when Herschel stuffed the pillow sack down his throat.

Thompson dipped the needle in a vial and filled the syringe. He held the needle in front of Hitler and said, "From your associate, Dr. Mengele. Bottoms up, *Mein Führer*." He plunged the needle into Hitler's neck and jammed the green substance into his veins.

It only took a few seconds for Hitler's pale face to flush bright red. His eyes watered and turned bloodshot, darting around as if to escape his skull. He screamed, but the pillowcase muffled his yells to a dull rapturous howl.

Only when Hitler defecated his pants did everyone let go. He scorned to retaliate, yet there was nothing he could do except die in anguish. His heart stopped after just over a minute. The last thing he ever saw were the vengeful Jews who put him down like a dog.

CHAPTER 39

VON SCHWANGAU COULD NOT HEAR his victims' blood-curdling screams through the periscope. He didn't have to. The poor bastards' expressions screamed louder than anything.

He always took particular pleasure in his service to the Reich, whether it was winning a battle, or merely sinking a lone enemy ship. The eruption of water, fire, and bodies upon impact of a torpedo made for a spectacular show, and it was his pleasure alone to view as U-1055's commander.

But his sentiments would shift on the afternoon of January 15, 1944, when he directed his men sink a British merchant ship in the English Channel. He tracked the phosphorus bubbles in the water as the torpedo sprang free of its firing tube and raced toward the vessel. Seeing the men realize they were about to be hit always proved interesting, and as typical, many jumped overboard preemptively.

The torpedo struck the ship dead center and rattled it with such tremendous force, it cracked clean in half. The men scurried to lifeboats in a last-ditch attempt, only to trample each other in the process.

One token lifeboat got free into the ice-cold seas, and no sooner than it cast away, a horse escaped its enclosure and jumped off the wreck. The creature plummeted at least thirty feet before it hit the lifeboat and sunk it in a crushing mess of gore. Von Schwangau didn't care to watch for the sharks. He'd seen more than he bargained for that day.

———

Raindrops splattered against Von Schwangau's mask- a trickling wakeup to the worst headache of his life. The Jew's point-blank lead didn't just concuss him; it briefly stopped his heart outright. He was only revived by that parting kick to his chest, a paradox he wouldn't soon waste.

It was just before dawn. He staggered to his feet and braced against a tree. His vision was so blurry that it reduced everything to a whirly green mess. Only when he shed his iron mask and relieved himself with his water canteen did the scenery stop spinning.

The tropical rain washed against his deformed face. He took a deep breath through two slits of a disintegrated nose and then opened his eyes. He bent down and collected his mask off the dirt, staring at a severe dent between the eye slits. He'd have to thank the welder for his master craftsmanship when this was all over.

Then he remembered: The village came under attack.

He slid the mask back over his face and latched the straps tight around his head. He looked about the ground and found his crossbow in the brush.

"Fools," he muttered to himself, dusting it off. He couldn't believe his enemies would be so careless as to leave him his weapon. It meant they really did fancy him dead.

His quiver was just a few feet away. He loaded a bolt in the draw and swung the device around his back. How long he'd been unconscious, he couldn't say. Perhaps he'd return to find the Jews' bodies prominently hanging from the village outskirts. He quietly hoped just one was still alive out there. This had already been his most thrilling hunt to date. To end on such a sour note would be an utter travesty.

Pain radiated throughout his head. He lost his footing and put a weak hand to his mask. Again, the trees started spinning. He ripped off his mask, fell to his knees, and vomited all over an ant hill. He watched the insects crawl out of his puke, only to embellish and carry away the morsels to their lair.

He got back on his feet and imbibed another gulp from his canteen. He thirsted for a cigarette, unusual since he'd given it up after the steam accident. The gaping holes in his face were crevices for smoke to escape, and although the majority of his nerves were dulled, smoking caused pain he could feel all too well. He wiped his dry lips and put his mask back on to continue at a slower pace. He took deep breaths to remedy the headache.

The sound of his intense huffing frightened the wildlife to silence. He maintained a zombie-like pace, oxygenating his brain to the point of euphoria and occasionally sipping on his canteen until it ran empty.

When he saw thin black smoke trailing through the trees, he stopped. Fear blossomed as he broke into a frenzied sprint. Moist air rushed through the eyeholes of his mask and wisped in his ears. Branches slapped against the iron, Von Schwangau paying no mind as he dashed for home.

He stopped when he broke free of the tree line. Scores of dead desecrated the village perimeter. The buzzing flies were louder than the jungle itself. Most of the buildings had been incinerated. The nets were gone, too, and blanketing the village had been no easy task. Doing it again after so many casualties would be another challenge entirely.

"*Oberführer* Von Schwangau!" he heard. He whirled around to see two boys carrying the dead body of a third. Von Schwangau recognized the casualty to be Paul. He remembered the boy aboard his U-boat at the tender age of six. He'd endured so much to flee, and now he would never see the Reich's rebirth. The boys couldn't tell, but a fierce scowl appeared beneath Von Schwangau's mask.

"What happened?" Von Schwangau demanded.

"We were ambushed," said one. "They came at us from either side and rescued their friend."

"They were successful?" Von Schwangau clarified in disbelief.

"Four squads are searching for them and the *Führer* as we speak, and *Oberführer* Gerhard has taken to the skies."

Von Schwangau gawked. "What do you mean 'them and the *Führer*?!'"

The boys exchanged fearful looks having to bear the news.

"The *Führer* is missing, sir. And, um..." The boy fell silent, looking to the other for help.

"Out with it," Von Schwangau snapped.

"It's the U-boat, sir. The intruders sunk it in the lake."

Von Schwangau's fists squeezed so tightly that he almost broke his own hands. Fury did not even come close to describing his rage.

"And, sir," the boy squeaked. "*Reichsmarschall* Mengele is nowhere to be found and all the other *Oberführers* are dead. You're the ranking commander."

"Put down those shovels," Von Schwangau said. "We will bury our dead and rebuild tomorrow. Have everyone stop what they're doing and go grab a gun."

CHAPTER 40

VADIM WIPED his tired eyes in disbelief at the growling Puma. He took out his snub nose .38 and pointed it.

"Don't," Thompson said, putting his hand over Vadim's gun.

"Unless I'm really that jumbled right now, there's a giant angry cat, Thompson. And it sure looks hungry," Vadim said.

The Puma lowered its stance to bear fangs and hiss.

"Luckily it appears to be looking at you, and not me," Vadim said. He holstered his .38 and politely stepped aside. "Better do something quick."

"Come together and stare it down," Thompson said. The group huddled close. Thompson bent down and scooped up a small stone. He tossed it at the cat and yelled.

The puma whined and swiped a defensive paw.

"You're pissing it off," Vadim said.

Thompson stomped and raised his arms above his head. He picked up another stone and hurled it. The puma had no idea what to do. It just hissed and then scurried away.

"That's funny. I never took you for an animal lover," Vadim said.

"Eyes open in case it decides to come back," Thompson cautioned.

They resumed pilgrimage without further ado. Their grimy clothes were so pungent, even the mosquitos elected to leave them alone. Everyone except Nadir was crashing hard from the Pervitin, but its after-effects were still potent enough to keep alert. Their minds were a different story, however- *"ridden hard and put away wet,"* as Thompson's mother used to say.

The Amazon river came into earshot shortly after daybreak. Thompson figured they were within one kilometer of the extraction point.

They emerged through the trees onto the river bank. The expansive waters flowed at a strong but manageable pace for when they would have to get in.

"I think we ought to brief General Fink as soon as we can," Bar-Yochai said. "Once those krauts realize we're gone for good, they might abandon this place."

"Let's just hope my photos are intact," Vadim said. "I think Fink's going to have a tough time believing all this, even with proof."

"Where are you going?" Thompson asked as Vadim strolled off toward the water.

"Relieving myself. Unless you care to watch?"

"Go," Thompson sighed.

Vadim unzipped his fly and contributed to the river's flow, eyes rolling back in his head with an exhale of relief. He opened them to stare up at the trees. If it weren't for circumstances, he might consider the place beautiful. Almost.

"Hurry it up," Thompson called.

"Almost done," Vadim said. Despite the jungle buzz, he thought he heard a voice singing in German.

Vadim peered around. There was nobody in sight, and the instant he diverted his attention, the singing stopped.

Leave it to Thompson to poison us with amphetamines, Vadim thought. He attributed it to an after effect of Pervitin and paid no further mind, shifting his gaze back down. But the sight of his penis was obstructed by a shiny metal bolt protruding from his chest. He put his finger to the bolt and pulled away to see it splotched red. His heed for warning didn't even have a chance to leave his lips. He splashed face down into the river, dead.

Thompson heard the sound and went to investigate. Vadim was nowhere to be seen until he adjusted his gaze and saw his friend floating away, the bolt protruding from him like a shark's fin. The camera film in Vadim's bag was well beyond salvation.

Then the singing resumed. Thompson looked across the river bank to see Von Schwangau standing with his crossbow in hand, having already loaded a fresh bolt in the arrow track. He squeezed the trigger and sent a bolt flying at Thompson.

The arrow skirted the brush and thudded against a tree.

"Run!" Thompson screamed. "It's the mask!"

They all took off. The Germanic verses from Von Schwangau's song followed through the trees like a disembodied voice. Meanwhile, arrow bolts sprinkled down in their wake. They couldn't even retreat far into the forest before Nazi gunfire cut them off.

"Where's Vadim?!" Nadir asked.

"*Es geht um Deutschlands Gloria, Gloria, Gloria. Sieg Heil! Sieg Heil Viktoria! Sieg Heil, Viktoria!*"

"Dead!" Thompson shouted as he took out his 1911. He unloaded it on the Nazi battalion approaching through the forest.

Bullets crisscrossed from all directions. Another arrow bolt ripped through the leaves and thunked into the tree they were hiding behind.

"They're cutting us off!" Bar-Yochai yelled.

Everyone's ammunition was dangerously low- maybe forty bullets for the entire lot of them, and the Nazis were like killer bees with a broken hive and a missing queen. They broke free from the trees and ran alongside the river shedding everything that weighed them down- empty guns, machetes, even their backpacks.

An arrow bolt landed smack in the mud and sent everyone diving in different directions. Thompson recovered his footing first. Despite the gunfire, he helped everyone up.

Von Schwangau pursued from the opposite side of the river bank. On their side, no less than fifty Nazis spilled out from the trees firing their guns indiscriminately.

Thompson fired three shots, ejected the magazine, and then slapped in his last one. A few Nazis dropped from his shots, but the rest kept charging.

An arrow bolt caught Thompson right through the shoulder and knocked him back into the mud. Blood leaked all over as he struggled to pull himself up. Another arrow bolt landed between his legs.

Herschel and Bar-Yochai came to Thompson's rescue, firing every last bullet they had. While Herschel helped Thompson up, Bar-Yochai issued cover fire from his Beretta.

Herschel yelped as hot Nazi bullet tore into his right bicep. He winced for just a moment before he looked back and gawked.

Everyone else turned to see what Herschel stared at, only to manifest similar faces of horror.

The P-39's guns blazed as it dipped low over the river. Water exploded in the wake of its bullets. Nadir was right in its path.

Thompson tackled her out of the way just as bullets shredded by. They had zero time to recover. The fighter lifted to bend back for another pass.

Von Schwangau loaded a fresh arrow bolt and aimed. Minus the one he'd picked off from across the river, he'd mostly been firing guess-shots at a forty-five-degree angle. But the hunt had to end. He could see the *Führer* wasn't with them. What that would mean for the Reich going forward, only time would tell.

Von Schwangau grinned when he skewered the one who shot him through the shoulder. But then his smile vanished upon realizing what the Jews were fleeing to:

In the middle of the river, the water's flow obstructed around the smallest conning tower Von Schwangau had ever seen. An American holding a large caliber rifle stood atop the tower.

"They're escaping!" he shouted in German. "Stop them! Those Jews-"

"Jews" would be his final words. Von Schwangau dropped the crossbow as a rifle bullet plunged through his right eye slit. His brains were blown out into the river, rendering one of the most dangerous naval minds of all time nothing but fish food.

CHAPTER 41

THE FIRING BOLT-ACTION Winchester rifle was the sweetest sound anyone in Nesher Unit had ever heard. Standing atop the tiny conning tower, a broad-shouldered Central Intelligence operative fired six shots at the Nazis. Then he dipped below the conning tower and emerged holding a life preserver. He threw the circular inflatable like a frisbee onto the river bank.

Herschel reached the life preserver first. He took hold of the inflatable and waded into the water, shielding Nadir with Bar-Yochai and Thompson. The three shoved Nadir onto the inflatable and covered her with their bodies. Nazi bullets pelted the water all around them.

"Pull us in!" Herschel shouted. He shrieked as another bullet tore into his thigh.

They kicked out into the river. Thompson let out a horrible yelp a few yards in. Pieces of his ear splattered onto the preserver and washed away with a splash. Blood spilled from the right side of his head where the bullet took his ear off.

They looked back to see the fighter dip down for another pass. They were helpless sitting ducks.

The fighter's guns erupted to send a track of bullets racing at them. If they let go of the inflatable, the river would sweep them away.

They all locked eyes. If these were their final moments, none could think of a better way to spend them.

Gerhard practically skimmed the river in desperation for the kill. He always maintained a masterful eye in the sky. However, jetting less than ten feet above the water at four-hundred miles per hour was difficult by any pilot's standards. He failed to see the small conning tower protruding from the water, or that he was perfectly lined up with the Central Intelligence operative.

Three cracks rang out from his Winchester. On the last shot, the fighter took a hit dead center in the propeller. The .30-06 copper-jacketed lead split on impact and savaged the engine.

Smoke filled the cockpit and blinded Gerhard's aim. His bullets missed by a hair. He tried to pull up, but as the plane angled fifty degrees, the propeller stopped spinning. Then the controls shorted out, frying the ejection mechanism.

The smoking fighter dropped like a stone and crashed over the hill. A massive fireball and accompanying boom signified Nesher Unit had one less name on their hit list.

The Central Intelligence operative took a .9mm bullet to the shoulder pulling in the inflatable. He dropped his rifle but kept pulling anyway. Another .9mm bullet tore through into his hip. He still didn't yield. On the third bullet to the arm, he fell into the conning tower. Two more operatives emerged to take his place.

Everyone held tight as they were dragged into the miniature submersible like a fresh fish catch. The water shimmied with missing gunfire. All except Nadir bore numerous wounds, and bullets still pinged the craft like a hail storm.

Nadir was first inside the submersible. Then the badly-bleeding Bar-Yochai and Herschel, and finally Thompson, who took one more bullet to the butt as he slipped in.

The steel hatch slammed shut, and the tiny submarine slipped below the waters.

The Nazis kept firing long after the craft vanished. Some even tried to swim after it. Others held back, accepting their fight was finally lost.

THE TRAIN SHUDDERED as it emerged from a tunnel onto a steep mountain bend. Nadir stared out the window at the abyss below, at least a thousand feet down, she judged. She saw an ocean of fall-tinted trees covering the ground as far as the eye could see.

"How's the tea?" Nadir heard someone ask. She looked over. Her mother sat opposite, dressed in her finest synagogue attire.

Nadir looked down at an old teacup filled to the brim with a dark red liquid. She brought the cup to her lips and tipped it back. "Strong," she said making a hard face.

"It's good for you," her mother replied. "You've got to take better care of yourself, Nadir. It's the most important thing."

"I know," Nadir said, sipping the tea despite her taste buds begging her to stop.

"You let these things come creeping in. There's no good in that. Are you listening?" she scolded when she observed Nadir staring back out the window.

"Where are we going?" Nadir asked.

"To the next stop," Nadir's mother said, taking out a cigarette.

"You smoke? Since when?"

"Your father and I are always trying new things with the time," she said, the cigarette wobbling in her lips as she lit it. "We do miss you terribly, though."

"I miss you too." She stared out the window again. "Wait a minute. Where exactly are we?"

Her mother ignored her. "They're a fine bunch of boys, Nadir. You found some very nice Jewish men. The two of us couldn't be happier."

"No, it's not like that, mom. They're my-"

The compartment door opened. Nadir's father entered holding a chess set. He closed the door sat next to Nadir's mother, where he began setting up the chess board.

"You want to play? Now?" she asked him.

Her father didn't reply. He finished setting up and then moved his white pawn to B6.

Nadir placed a hand on her knight, but before she could lift it, the train jerked forward as the brakes screamed. She could see they were coming into a station on the mountain's side. Uzziel and Vadim stood together on the platform.

"Too bad," her father said.

She looked forward. The chess board vanished. Her father sipped tea instead. "You're too skilled for me anyway, my little *Feygele*," he said, reaching over to pinch her cheek. "I'm afraid this is your stop."

"But I don't want to get off."

"You'll get back on eventually. Everyone does, one day. Now let's go greet your friends," her father said, ushering her onto the platform.

The mountain seemed infinitely, no *impossibly* high. She could see the train tracks wrapped endlessly all the way up beyond the clouds.

Vadim held a bag stuffed with art supplies in his left hand, and a blank canvas in his right. Uzziel looked dressed for combat. His tactical vest was covered in firearms small and large. He clipped a silver pistol free of his ensemble, popped a single bullet out of the chamber, and caught it mid-air.

"Keepsake," he said, pocketing the bullet. He handed the gun to Nadir and added, "Don't miss."

The train whistle screamed. A conductor cried, "All aboard!"

"Gentlemen," Nadir's father said, gesturing to Uzziel and Vadim.

"Wait!" Nadir shouted.

The train whistle sounded again, this time dissolving to a voice that said, "Nadir."

Nadir looked down at Uzziel's handgun. When she saw her reflection in the gun's gleam, the look on her face was a shattering blow. She suddenly realized none of it was real.

That's when she sat up with a gasp.

It had been two weeks since she returned to Rafa's home in Chicago, and she hadn't heard a shred of news. The submersible exodus down the river had been nothing short of terrifying. Everyone except her bled like stuffed pigs, and if they died shielding her, she'd never forgive herself.

But Adonai was with them. The submersible escaped the Amazon and rendezvoused with an American destroyer off the coast. A Piasecki HUP transport waited on deck to fly the injured away. It marked the last time she'd seen any of her comrades.

"Heavens!" Rafa cried. "You nearly gave me a heart attack."

Nadir fell flat on the bed and put a hand to her damp forehead.

"You don't have to say much to say a lot, child. I know better than to ask, but based on your friend's new injury, I'd say you've been through the woods. Perhaps have some gin before you sleep tonight, mmm?"

Nadir sat up again. "Wait, Thompson's here?"

"Yes, he's downstairs. An ear less than when I saw him last. I think it looks good on him. Gives character. Tell him I said that, would you?"

Rafa excused himself for Nadir to dress. When she got downstairs, Thompson looked almost unrecognizable. He was clean-shaven, with a fresh military haircut. But he walked with crutches and his arm was still in a sling, and when he turned his head, he revealed deformity. It was slightly unsettling to see her friend so severely battle-scarred.

"Rafa's right. It does give you character," she said.

Thompson chuckled. "I like that. My mother's furious. Good thing she doesn't know I have a tiny tattoo on my right ass cheek. That'd put her right in the ground, her only son running around with *Goy* markings."

"Luckily, we don't have a corpse for her to identify," Nadir said. "Are you okay? It doesn't hurt?"

"Nah. Doctors are working on making a prosthetic, and if ever there was a cause to lose an ear for..." he trailed off. "Everyone's going to be okay, Nadir, even the one who saved our ass with the rifle. He got hit pretty bad, but he's alive. He also confirmed the mask's death."

"Who was he?"

"Kurtz Von Schwangau, a U-boat captain presumed sunk at the end of the war." Thompson looked around for Rafa's prying ears. "Can we talk privately in the basement?"

It wasn't an outrageous request. Although Rafa knew to steer clear of Nadir's work, a retired old man who seldom left home was privy to whatever entertainment entered his domicile.

Nadir led Thompson out of the room, where she heard Rafa skulking down the hall. She glanced back at Thompson. He smiled and shook his head.

They descended into an unfinished basement filled with boxes. Nadir flicked on a single overhead light and posted up against a box stack.

"There were a lot of names in that village we didn't even know were out there. What did Fink say when you told him who we found?"

Thompson averted his eyes.

"Wait. You didn't tell him?"

"Fink got what he needed to hear. I told him we found a commune of fugitives planning post-war retribution with a stolen a-bomb. We swore Hitler would die forgotten in those woods. The truth is ours alone to bear."

"I understand," Nadir said. "If Uzziel and Vadim were here, I'm sure they would have agreed too. So, what did Fink do? We lost the camera with all the evidence."

"The Nazi lead in our bodies was all the proof we needed. Bastards even had swastikas carved into most of the bullets. The intelligence spooks backed up what we saw, too. Fink sent a twenty-man special ops team in last week, but by the time they got there, the compound was abandoned. They didn't even bury the dead. However, the team did manage to recover the bomb from the lake, and they found this." Thompson took out Rafa's Browning and handed it over.

"You actually got it back?"

"They inventoried all the guns they found. Everything was German. So, when I saw they logged a Browning, I had a feeling."

"I'm glad you got it back, but it still doesn't change things. We didn't get 'em all, Thompson. A bunch still managed to slip away. We failed."

"Quite the opposite, and don't you ever think like that again. Thanks to us, the Reich is dead, and Nesher Unit proved its worth beyond a shadow of a doubt."

"But we're shrinking fast. Pretty soon we're the ones who will get cycled out. Then what?"

"Perhaps that's the direction Nesher Unit needs to go. We were General Fink's experiment that worked. He kept Budapest off the President's desk, but you can bet Fink shared this. The President took note, Nadir. Not just of what we did, but of you."

"Me?" she said. "Why?"

"You escaped enemy capture. You supplied intel that led to the seizure of a Soviet nuclear weapon. You killed Dr. Mengele and Klaus Barbie, and you even sank an enemy vessel."

"Bar-Yochai sank it," Nadir said.

"Not according to him, he didn't." It was a rarity to see

Thompson leak such emotion. Even his eyes were glossy. "All I can say to you is *Mazel Tov*. You really are something else."

An overpowering blush flushed Nadir's cheeks red. "You'd have done the same thing."

Thompson shook his head. "This was only your second time in the field. If there's one thing you've proved, it's that you are not to be underestimated. That's why I'm here. Not just to debrief you, but to appoint you going forward."

"Appoint me?"

Thompson took out a small velvet box and flipped it open to reveal a golden badge that bore a Star of David with an eagle in the middle. "We're not the same shadow group anymore. This is our new official seal. The President wants to expand Nesher Unit, and you're going to command. I'm stepping down."

"What?! Why?!"

"Because I can't bury another friend, Nadir. I'll die alongside one just fine, but I can't be the one who issues death orders."

"I'm flattered, but I'm not qualified. Not like Bar or Hersch are."

"Both you and Vadim wanted to abort, and if only I'd listened..." Thompson paused. "I talked it over with Bar and Hersch in the hospital. They agree this is the right move," he said, pushing the badge forward.

Nadir took it out and held it in her hands. "It's beautiful."

"Vadim designed it. I found it last week going through one of his old sketchbooks."

"I don't know what to say. I'm... honored. Thank you."

"Nadir, listen to me. We might not have apprehended everyone, but under your leadership, I don't have a doubt we will. Congratulations... commander." Thompson saluted her.

"I won't let you down," Nadir said, returning the salute. She closed the box and held it close to her heart. "Are Bar and Herschel able to walk yet?"

"Herschel got hit pretty bad. He might need a few more weeks, but Bar's back on his feet. There will be plenty of time to visit them both after your meeting in D.C." he said.

"I'm flying to D.C.?" she asked.

"Yes, you and General Fink are meeting with the President at noon tomorrow. My advice? You had best acquire a taste for golf, and quick," Thompson said. "Come on. Let's go upstairs, and I'll walk you through what to expect."

"Will you be coming too?" she asked.

"As far as the runway, but no further. You're the commander. This is your affair now," Thompson said. "But rest assured, anything you need, the three of us will always be there for you."

Somewhere in Rafa's dusty basement, there was a box filled with heirlooms of the long-departed Horowitz family. Among its treasures were photos of a family shattered, remnants of normality scourged by the plague of nationalism. The last living person in the photos, Nadir, closed the door and shuttered the basement in darkness. Though the rest of the people in those old photos could no longer smile, nor hear, nor feel with beating hearts, from beyond the grave, their spirits beamed.

ACKNOWLEDGMENTS

First and foremost, I want to thank Joe. You courageously serve your community as a paramedic and you've showed me undying kindness that I won't ever forget.

To David and the entire Kuettel Family. Thank you for help illustrating the cover and all your years of love, kindness, and friendship.

To thank my parents, Harold and Carroll. You've stood behind me and supported me, even when it seemed like my writing was going nowhere.

To my Beta Readers- particularly Ian and Joe– thank you for the notes.

To Ms. Gens, my eleventh-grade history teacher. Your World War II lectures gave me the genesis for this story so many years ago.

To all my best friends in life and to everyone I do martial arts with- you are a muse that inspires me so.

To the rest of my extended Britton family, and to my aunt, Sally Kail.

And- most importantly - to my readers. Thank you for taking time out of your life to give my hard work your attention. Nesher Unit will return for another installment... One day.

ABOUT THE AUTHOR

Evan Kail was raised Jewish in the Minnesotan suburb of Edina and earned a bachelor's degree in Japanese studies from the University of Minnesota. He is passionate about martial arts and currently holds the rank of third-degree black belt in taekwondo, and first dan in kumdo. He is also a mixed-media artist and author of the nonfiction book series, *Ubered*.

Wolf in the Jungle is Evan's first fiction title, and he plans to release many more in the coming years, both fiction and non-fiction. Follow him on social media @evankail for more updates about his upcoming writing projects.

Made in the USA
Monee, IL
20 April 2021